DEATH BY PRIDE

A Kyle Callahan Mystery

Mark McNease

Copyright 2014 Mark McNease

MadeMark Publishing
New York City
www.mademarkublishing.com

ISBN-10: 0-9916279-3-8
ISBN-13: 978-0-9916279-3-6

All rights reserved. No part of this book may be reproduced or transmitted in any form or by any means, electronic or mechanical, including photocopying, recording, or by any information storage and retrieval system, without permission in writing from the publisher.

This book is a work of fiction. Names, characters, places, situations and incidents are the product of the author's imagination or are used fictitiously. Any resemblance to actual events, locales, or persons living or dead is purely coincidental.

For Frank Murray

*May you always answer my knock
at the top of the stairs.*

1

Killing wasn't as much fun as it used to be. He expected to be a bit rusty after three years, but he had never anticipated this ... *dullness*, this sense that, in the words of bluesman B.B. King, the thrill was gone. Maybe he had just been away from it too long; maybe he needed to get up to speed. The man whose body he deposited into the East River just before midnight was, after all, only the first in his current series. There would be two more before the week was out, and maybe the old rush would return with the next one. He had to trust it would, to believe as a child believes that Santa Claus is real and will come shimmying down the chimney every Christmas Eve. Or how Dorothy believed, clicking her slippers in that dreadful movie. That might be a more appropriate comparison, given the occasion. Click, click, click ... and he was home.

He did not come all the way back to New York to resume his annual ritual for something as lackluster as this first kill. Had it been the young man himself whose death stirred so little response in him? What was his name? Victor? Victor Someone. Dense and inattentive; he had been too easy, and far too handsome. *Cute*, really. The kind of cute that becomes very sexual in manhood. Innocent smile, calculated shyness. Victor Someone knew exactly what he was doing flirting in the store that afternoon, and he had succeeded, much to his regret.

Unfortunately, Victor wasn't nearly as enjoyable to kill as he was to look at. Too easy, too unchallenging. Like a cat who had no trouble capturing a wingless bird, he had not had fun with this one. He would have to analyze the experience, figure out why it had not been as satisfying as it was before, and what he might need to do to reignite his excitement. Did he need to be more brutal? Did he need to introduce tools into the game, a scalpel, perhaps, or a drill of some kind? He would think hard on it. A decision had to be made quickly; he'd already placed an online ad looking for the next one and the emails were flooding into his special account, the one no one would ever trace no matter how hard they tried. A phantom as elusive as he was deserved a phantom email routed through Chicago, then London and Tokyo, server after server erasing any clue to its origin.

Deidrich Kristof Keller III—D to everyone who knew him well (a thought that made him chuckle, since the only ones who truly knew him died with the knowledge) had only been back in his townhouse since March. His tenants, the ones he rented to when he left for Berlin to take care of his mother, had a lease through February and D had waited patiently for them to leave. A lovely young couple with two small children. He'd never met Susan and Oliver Storch—the rental had been arranged through an agent—but they had taken very good care of the place, he would give them that. And you would never know they had children; no stray toys were left behind, no evidence, really, that anyone had been there at all for the past three years. His kind of people.

He was so glad to be back. He'd hated Berlin, all of Germany for that matter, though he saw very little of it and had no desire to see more. For D being German was as meaningless as someone being Scottish who had never been to Scotland, spoke with no brogue, and was only tied to the land by name and ancestry. His parents were from Germany, but they had moved to Anaheim, California, before D was born. His mother, Marta, returned to Berlin a broken, bitter woman, but that was not his fault. She was a coward. *Cowardess?* he wondered, making a cup of tea at his kitchen counter. It was an island counter, surrounded by a stove and refrigerator large enough to impress and too large to be practical—there was almost nothing in the refrigerator, and he rarely cooked. The entire townhouse was furnished for show—the furniture, the artwork, the paintings and photographs of nonexistent family members and forebears. It had been carefully put together to deceive. Anyone who came into his home would think he was just another wealthy man in New York City with a long lineage, should one wonder where he came from. Men with paintings of their grandfathers above a fireplace surely belonged in Manhattan's upper reaches and had unquestionable pedigree. That was the point, to be unquestioned. By the time anyone got around to questioning him, to wondering about his authenticity, it was too late. He answered their questions with a belt around their necks. The belt he kept especially for them. *You're right, good man, I'm not who I appear to be. Please keep that to yourself.* And they did.

He was tired now. He'd worked out how to get the bodies out of his house unnoticed some years ago, but he was getting older, forty-two this coming September. It wasn't as easy as it used to be. And this one had been heavier than he'd guessed when he chose him.

Note to self: never, ever, pick a customer from the store again. No matter how cute or handsome, no matter how liquid and shining the eyes or seductive the smile. Stay online, stay hidden behind a dozen re-routers, change names each time, do not take this risk ever again.

He'd been away too long, losing his edge in his mother's dreary Berlin apartment, saving himself for his return to the killing ground. He'd have to sharpen quickly; mistakes were something other people made. He'd made one this time—the only time in all his successes—and he would not make another one.

He would look at Victor Someone's driver's license in the morning. Sense memory was a beautiful thing, and nothing brought it back quite like his keepsakes. The license was his souvenir—his thirteenth. Lucky thirteen. The rest of the wallet stayed with the body. He wasn't interested in making identification difficult. It didn't matter if the police knew who had been killed, only that they would never find the man who did the killing.

It had been dark when he parked by the river. The new moon had worked to his favor, a first. No one had been around; he made sure no one saw a man with a heavy, strangely shaped object wrapped in black plastic trudging his way to the river's edge. Then a simple heave and splash, and he was on his way home.

Bedtime at last. But before then, for a few minutes anyway, he wanted to go through those emails. He'd requested photos, knowing many of them would be old and meant to trick him, and that was okay. He was less interested in finding a man who looked exactly like his picture than he was in finding a man who made him want to kill. It was like falling in love with an image: he never knew which one it would be, but knew it when it happened. *This one. Oh yes. This one will be here soon.*

He turned off the kitchen light, took his tea cup with the little chain from the tea ball hanging over the side, and headed to his large master bedroom on the second floor. His laptop was open and waiting for him. He would sift through a dozen or so email responses and see if any of them struck his fancy. But first, the pictures of Victor. Victor Someone. He would enjoy those before sleeping. He always took pictures.

2

Kyle Callahan loved being married, it was the *getting married* that had been such an ordeal. He'd been with his partner, Danny Durban, for just over seven years when they finally made it official—and legal, in the state of New York, at least. That had been one of the reasons they'd waited: neither of them would marry until they could do it in their home state. And now, with the Federal Government recognizing their marriage, there had been no reason to put it off any longer. So on May 12th, just six weeks ago, he and Danny had gone to City Hall in downtown Manhattan and gotten their license. The following Saturday they stood before seventy-five of their closest friends at Metropolitan Community Church and publicly declared their intention to spend the rest of their lives together. Danny had wanted the 12th as their wedding date, to honor the anniversary of their first meeting at the Katherine Pride Gallery, but it fell on a Tuesday. Nobody gets married on a Tuesday, at least not anyone with a mother-in-law flying in with her boyfriend from Chicago, another set of parents from Queens, siblings, nieces, bosses, and Kyle's best friend Detective Linda Sikorsky from New Jersey, along with her own newly minted wife Kirsten McClellan.

The sheer logistics of a wedding were more than Kyle or Danny had ever anticipated. It starts out simply enough as a vision in which all these friends, relatives and loved ones magically appear to celebrate the happy couple's bliss. In that first fantasy phase there are no hotels to recommend, no invitation list to cull, no feelings to hurt by being excluded from the guest list. And certainly no large pile of cash to drop for an affair that seemed to have $10,000 as its starting price. By the time they headed downtown for their license both men were frayed at the edges, ready to elope and send all these people a nice photograph instead. It was too late by then and the worst was over, so they went through with it and now would not have had it any other way. The cost only set them back three years' worth of prime vacation travel, but that was okay. It had been a huge success and they were finally married.

The inevitable let-down after so much stress, planning and execution had lasted about a week for Kyle, less for Danny who was busy dealing with the imminent departure of his beloved Margaret Bowman. Margaret had started Margaret's Passion, the restaurant Danny now owned with Kyle and Kyle's mother Sally. She'd hired Danny almost twelve years ago, then sold the restaurant to him last year as she crept into her 80s. Now, as he had dreaded, she was preparing to move to Florida to spend her remaining days with her sister Rebecca, leaving Margaret's Passion to Danny to fully make his own. As long as there was a Margaret's Passion there would be a Margaret, if only in photographs on the walls with the many celebrities and politicians she'd served so well and lovingly over the decades. But the thought of her being so far away and likely never to return had left Danny in a funk for months. His wedding, despite the rigors of it, the anxiety and the stress, was a high point and a needed distraction from the loss he faced. There would only be one wedding for both men; there would only be one Margaret Bowman, too, and having her there in the front row with their parents was a memory they would cherish as much as the wedding itself.

Kyle was thinking about it all as he scanned the previous day's mail at their kitchen table. It was his habit to get the mail when he got home in the early evening, but he'd been distracted and had forgotten, instead taking the elevator down to pick it up this morning, along with the New York Times that lay outside their door. In the age of online everything, Kyle still preferred reading the paper the old fashioned way—with pages that turned and ink that came off on his fingers.

The men lived on the edge of Gramercy Park, at Lexington Avenue and 25th Street. Danny could easily walk to Margaret's Passion just six blocks away, and Kyle could get to the Japan TV3 offices, where he worked as the personal assistant to firebrand and borderline has-been TV reporter Imogene Landis, with an easy bus ride and a cross town stroll. Their dear friend Detective Linda (now retired from the New Hope, Pennsylvania, police force) was asleep in the spare room, turning it once again from their shared office into a guest room. She'd come into town the day before for her first Pride weekend and parade and Kyle made plans for them to see the city in much more detail than Linda had been able to on her last visit. That was in late April a year ago, and she and Kyle had been caught up trying to stop the killer Kieran Stipling as he murdered his way through a list of people connected to the Katherine Pride Gallery. Whatever sightseeing Linda had planned that visit was abandoned in the race to end the killing. Kyle intended to make up for it this time.

Danny walked in wearing the plush brown robe Kyle gave him the previous Christmas. The smell of morning coffee always brought him out of the bedroom, trailed moments later by their cats, Smelly and Leonard.

"Linda awake yet?" he asked, heading straight to the coffee pot and taking a cup from the cabinet above it. The cats took up position at his feet, expecting early morning treats.

"I doubt it," Kyle said. "I think she was up late, I heard her talking on the phone just before I fell asleep."

"It's terrible about Kirsten's mother. I wish we could see her again."

"I'm sure Linda wishes it, too. We're at that age, Danny ..."

"I know, I know, let's not talk about it."

Time did not take sides, it only passed in a constant flow, and eventually the people we ride the stream with begin to fall off to the shore. Kyle's father had been gone over fifteen years. Margaret was heading off soon for a few good years in Florida before she, too, slipped from the stream. It wouldn't be long before their parents were gone and they took their place at the head of the line, saying goodbye to friends one by one—or perhaps saying goodbye themselves. Life makes no guarantees and takes no reservations.

Linda's wife Kirsten was in Phoenix with her dying mother. The women had hastily flown her to New Jersey in March and married in a very small ceremony in Stockton with just Kyle, Danny, and the women's mothers in attendance. It was the kind of wedding Kyle envied after the ordeal of his own. The next day Kirsten flew back with her mother and had been spending weeks at a time travelling back and forth. Her mother, Dot McClellan, had cancer metastasized throughout her body and was not expected to see the end of July. Linda's plan was to enjoy this weekend in the city with Kyle and Danny, then head to Phoenix. It had taken a serious toll on both women, and Kyle noticed how much thinner Linda was when she'd arrived yesterday afternoon.

They'd met Detective Linda Sikorsky a year and a half ago during Halloween weekend at Pride Lodge. The Lodge sat on twenty-five acres near the Delaware River, on the Pennsylvania side. Kyle's friend and lodge handyman, Teddy Pembroke, had been found dead at the bottom of the lodge's empty pool, and Linda was the homicide detective investigating the death, which proved to be deliberate. Murder, it seemed, was their first commonality, but since then they'd found many more. Kyle and Linda spoke every few days, and last fall he and Danny spent a week at her small house in the woods in Hunterdon County, New Jersey. Linda had inherited the house from her aunt Celeste and, with some reluctance, moved from her longtime home in New Hope to take up residence with the deer, rabbits and strange sounds nature makes when it has no competition. The highlights of the visit were supposed to be a week of sightseeing, country living and good food at fine local restaurants; instead, it became a hunt for the killer of Abigail Creek, matriarch of CrossCreek Farm and victim of a vicious hit-and-run. Their time together always seemed to attract murderers—or the other way around—and sometimes Kyle wondered if they should just maintain a long-distance friendship, in the interest of keeping people alive.

"Did you see Vinnie when you picked up the mail this morning?" Danny asked, stirring creamer into his coffee and taking it to the table. He sat next to Kyle and picked up the mail, flipping through it so see what was his. Leonard stayed in the kitchen, staring up at the coffee pot as if he could not understand there were no treats in it for him. Smelly, the wiser of the two, followed Danny to the table and perched at his feet, knowing he would eventually relent and get the pouch of fish-flavored nuggets for her.

"Come to think of it, no. The relief guy was on duty, what's his name?"

"Dayton."

"Dayton? That's an unusual name."

The building had doormen. It was a perk Kyle had never known before moving from Brooklyn into Danny's apartment. It took a while to get used to, but not too long. Having someone open the door for you and receive packages and visitors was luxurious without being too elitist. Vinnie—Vincent Campagna—had the overnight shift and was among the most reliable doormen the building had ever had. He was in his mid-thirties, and in ten years on the door had not been off more than three or four times. This was the second night he'd called in.

"Is Vinnie sick?" Kyle asked, scanning the paper. The city's new mayor was making changes, many of which were controversial and demanded above-the-fold coverage.

"No, it's some family thing," Danny said. "Something about his brother missing, I'm not sure. There's not that much communication between tenants and the doormen, but I've heard things in the elevator."

Kyle kept reading the paper. The mayor was pushing for some new legislation, the mayor was insisting on a vote his way by the City

Council, the U.S. Congress was at a stalemate again. He flipped the paper over to see what news hadn't made it to the top ... and he froze. An article just below the fold was headlined, "Man Found in East River Identified, Police Searching for Clues."

Kyle started reading the story.

"You know, I think Smelly's finally losing weight," Danny said, looking down at the cat. She had been pre-diabetic for several years, but every effort at trimming her down had failed. "Maybe it's age."

"Shh!" Kyle said, focused on the article

"What's so interesting that you have to 'shhh' me?"

Kyle ignored him, reading. "What is Vinnie's last name?" he said after a moment.

"Campagna. Vincent Campagna."

"He has a brother."

"Yes."

"A brother who's also a doorman."

"Yes. I think their father was, too. A family tradition I guess, like the military. What are you reading? Is Vinnie in the news?"

"No, he's not," Kyle said, sliding the paper to the side. "But his brother, Victor, is."

"In a good way, I hope," Danny said, reaching for the paper to read about it himself.

"Not at all. In a bad way. A very bad way."

Danny read the article quickly. "Oh my God," he said.

"Oh my God is right. Victor Campagna is the body they found in the river Tuesday morning. You saw the story."

"It was everywhere. But nothing about it being an accident or a murder."

"This is awful."

Smelly began meowing, an escalation of her demands for a treat. Kyle swatted her away with his free hand.

"He's back," Kyle said.

Danny looked up at him. The article hadn't named a suspect. "Who is 'he'?"

"The Pride Killer."

Danny remembered then. Every year for four years at Pride weekend the East River had become a depository for victims of a man—assuming it was a man—who remained uncaught. The media had dubbed him the Pride Killer, because the murders only happened that weekend in June, stopping once the festivities were over. Then radio silence. No killing, no bodies, nothing for another year, and another.

"Three years," Kyle said, as if he'd read Danny's thoughts. "He stopped three years ago and they couldn't figure out why. Everyone hoped he was dead, or that he'd come to his senses, if madmen have senses."

"But the paper doesn't say who—"

"It's him. The hands and feet bound, the strangulation, the location of the body. Even if it traveled in the current they'll trace it back to the general vicinity of where this guy dumps his bodies."

"Now we know why Vinnie hasn't been to work," Danny said. "He must be devastated."

"It says the body was found two nights ago. Poor Vinnie. And his family, I can't imagine."

The men grew silent. Smelly, sensing something was wrong, stopped her meowing and slinked off into the living room. She would get what she wanted, but later, when moods had returned to normal. Leonard was still staring at the coffee pot.

Finally, Kyle said, "He won't stop."

"How do you know that, if it's even him? He stopped for three years."

"Because this was the first. There will be a second, and a third. That's the way he works."

Danny had a sinking feeling. If timing was everything, it worked against them very well. Detective Linda visiting, a body in the East River; the stars had aligned in a way most displeasing to him as he watched Kyle's face for the telltale glazed expression, the speeding, clicking thoughts. He worried Kyle would not stay out of it, and that sooner or later something terrible would happen to them. They were married now, together forever. What happened to one of them, happened to both of them.

"Listen, Kyle …"

"Don't worry. This is one for the police."

Danny had the feeling he had just been lied to. Not deliberately; Kyle had every intention of staying out of it. But it was his nature to wonder—wonder who this man was taking the lives of other men, where he lived, how he found his victims. Danny knew that as much as Kyle might try to ignore this, it would take root in his mind and grow until he had to do something.

"What's cooking?" Detective Linda said, startling them both. Neither had heard her come out of the bedroom.

A sense of dread came over Danny as he blew across his coffee, cooling it. He knew Linda and Kyle would soon be lost in conversation about serial killers and floating bodies. Why can't his husband just be an amateur photographer and a personal assistant? Why must he take it upon himself to rid the world of bad people? Sooner or later one of those bad people might rid the world of Kyle.

3

She could hear the men in the living room ... or was it the kitchen? Living room, kitchen, entryway, they all seemed to flow into each other in Manhattan apartments, if Kyle and Danny's was a typical example. Linda Sikorsky had no way of knowing—she had not been in any other apartments in New York City, except for the penthouse she and Kyle had burst into just in time to stop Kieran Stipling from cutting Stuart Pride's throat. That was over a year ago, and still the memory of it gave her chills. She stretched on the sofa bed, letting the unpleasant thoughts evaporate as she reached up with her hands, stretched her arms, and pushed her toes down until they almost went over the end of the mattress.

So much had happened since those awful murders. Kyle and Danny had gotten married, an elaborate event to which Linda and Kirsten were witness along with dozens of other people. The women had stayed in a boutique hotel in Park Slope that catered to lesbians, and only overnight; they wanted the men to have time alone, as if seven years were not enough. And even though Kyle had protested, insisting they should stay a few days, Linda knew he was secretly happy to have them all gone. Weddings were intense affairs and while it had been glorious, Linda was glad she and Kirsten had taken a much more intimate approach. They'd had to; Kirsten's mother was living on borrowed time (or, Linda thought, dying on it), and circumstances demanded they move quickly.

Linda's personal life had experienced significant changes as well. She and Kirsten McClellan were living together now as wife and wife, tucked in the woods in Linda's small house. There'd been a rocky, unsure time, last fall when Kyle and Danny visited, but it had passed and things were as secure and comforting as Linda imagined they could be, back when she'd first said hello at a New Year's Eve party to the woman she now shared her life with. Back then Kirsten was a highly successful real estate agent in New Hope, long established with her own company, and infinitely more experienced with relationships than Linda. While Linda had had several relationships with men over her forty-four years and even once considered marrying in her twenties, she had never dated a woman. Now she was married to one.

Another big change since her last trip to Manhattan was retiring from the police force and opening her vintage-everything store. *For Pete's Sake* was named after her father, a cop whose senseless death when Linda was eight years old had left an indelible stain on her heart. It was why she'd become a police officer, and why she named her business after him. She had put in her twenty years on the force, the last five as a homicide detective, and had given her notice. On the last Friday in September, Detective Linda became just Linda Sikorsky. No more notifying the next of kin, no more days at the precinct, no more nights and weekends hoping her phone wouldn't ring, calling her to a crime scene. She loved being a cop, and making detective had been among her life's true high points. But she had gone into the career in large part because of her father and the time had come to move on and honor him in other ways.

She had known even as a child that her mother Estelle worried every moment Pete was on duty, and most that he was not. Pete Sikorsky was the kind of cop—the kind of man—who stepped in if he saw someone in trouble or if he thought he could stop evil in its many forms. It's what killed him, and why Estelle had been right to fret nearly every waking moment of their lives. Pete had gone to the small corner grocery store just three blocks from their house and, proving fate's capricious nature, walked into a robbery. He hadn't entered the store yet when two men who had just held up the grocer at gun point came bursting out of the door. A police cruiser that had been nearby came gunning up the street. One of the robbers fired, confusion ensued, and five seconds later Peter Sikorsky lay dying on the sidewalk, a stray bullet in his neck.

Several years later Estelle remarried and moved with her new husband and daughter to Philadelphia, where she now lived as a seventy-three-year-old double widow. Linda became a police officer, got a job with the New Hope force, and twenty-plus years later she had turned one of the biggest pages in her life. Her one advantage was knowing what she wanted to do "in retirement." Many people have no idea what to do with themselves when they leave a job they'd been at for over two decades; many a cop ended his life with a gun in his mouth, haunted by what he'd seen, usually divorced a time or two, and so lost he or she saw no way out of the tunnel but the bright light of a gun muzzle. Linda would not be one of them. She had long wanted to open a "vintage everything" store, modeled after her favorite shop in Doylestown, Pennsylvania. She'd even become friends with Suzanne, the store owner, and Suzanne had mentored her since the store's opening last November. The business had done well and Linda had even been able to hire an assistant manager, Mitchell Parsons. Mitch was in his fifties, a devoted gay bachelor and an even more devoted assistant manager who ran the store more efficiently than Linda ever could. He'd been a real find and she was relieved beyond words to have him back in New Hope taking care of the store now. With her mother-in-law dying in Phoenix and the frequent trips she and Kirsten were making there, having Mitch to take care of things was among the great comforts in Linda's life. She made a mental note to call him later this morning and see how things were going—if he didn't call her first to tell her, which was usually the case.

Kyle and Danny were sitting at the kitchen table when Linda joined them, wearing yellow silk pajamas with bright green parrots on them. She had picked them up on a trip to San Francisco with Kirsten for their honeymoon. They accentuated her long dark blonde hair. Linda Sikorsky was a tall woman, "big boned" as her mother always said. At five-nine she stood head to head with Kyle. When she'd been on duty, wearing her navy suit, a holster on her hip and a badge clipped to her breast pocket, she had presented an intimidating presence. Sometimes it worked in her favor, such as when she had to question suspects; other times it kept people from trusting and befriending her. She believed it was one of the reasons she had stayed single and closeted for so many years; not because she didn't accept herself, but because life was just easier, simpler, when you spent it alone. It was a feeling she hoped to never have again.

"What's cooking?" Linda said, shuffling into the kitchen.

"Nothing," Kyle replied. "We're going out for breakfast."

"No, not literally cooking. I wouldn't expect you to make me breakfast. I mean what's up. It's seven o'clock in the morning."

"We're up, obviously," Danny said, standing and heading to the sink. He took a coffee cup from the cabinet above it and handed it to Linda. "Kyle was just going through the mail, reading the paper."

"Anything interesting?"

"In the mail or the paper?"

"Either."

"Oh yes," Kyle said, and he tapped the newspaper with his finger. "Something very interesting indeed."

Linda got her coffee and joined Kyle at the table.

"Why are you so interested in this?" Danny asked. He did not sit back down. He planned to go back to the bedroom and watch the news, joined by Smelly and Leonard, each cat settling in on either side of him.

"Because it's Vinnie's brother."

Linda: "Who's Vinnie? What are you interested in?"

Having their doorman's brother found floating in the East River made it personal for Kyle.

"I didn't know you were friends with Vinnie," Danny said.

"I'm not *un*friendly. We talk. And think about it, Danny. If this could happen to Vinnie's brother, it could happen to anyone … and will. If this is the first victim, which I'm guessing it is, there are going to be two more. Two innocent men, right now going about their lives with no idea what's waiting for them."

"And what is that?" asked Linda.

"Not what," Kyle said, "but who."

Kyle began telling Linda about the unsolved murders linked to the Pride Killer, how he had struck every Pride weekend for four years, then vanished, and how now, with the death of their doorman's brother, he had managed to hit very close to home.

Danny left them to their conversation and headed to the bedroom, the cats following behind like large mice on a trail of cheese. He wanted nothing to do with serial killers and dead bodies in the river. He had hoped after the Pride Gallery murders and that terrible business at CrossCreek Farm their lives would stop intersecting with murder, but he knew his hope had been in vain. Trouble had a way of finding them, as if it had been patiently waiting just ahead for them to turn the corner. Then it stepped out from the shadows.

4

D sat luxuriating in the vastness of his king-sized bed, enjoying the quiet of the morning. The bedroom was in the corner of the townhouse's second floor and he could see the sun rising slowly over the river six blocks away. He had loved rivers all his life and would live on a riverbank if he could. If the rains came and flooded his riverbank home, he would stand in his living room with his legs in the water, marveling at the water's mystery and power, and if it swept him away he would glide along in its current, surrendered to going wherever it took him. He had no idea where this love came from—there had been no river in Anaheim when he was a child, no river near his uncle Leo's apartment in Brooklyn, where he'd gone to live when his mother fled back to Berlin in tatters. And it wasn't a general love of water; he was not fond of oceans or lakes. It was specific to rivers, something about rivers that moved his spirit in ways matched only by killing. He kept meaning to examine the connection between the two—a river's mighty flow as it followed its banks along channels carved in antiquity, and the mighty flow of his blood when he ended men's lives and commended their lifeless bodies to the very river he loved and respected so much. But he had no one with whom to examine this connection, no therapist to talk to, no close friend. So he had put it off and put it off, until he finally accepted he may never analyze or understand it. It just was.

He was careful not to drop crumbs on the sheets as he enjoyed his toasted corn muffin, his laptop open at his side. He had no housekeeper; inviting anyone at all into his home was a risk. He occasionally needed a plumber or an electrician, but he made sure they stayed in whichever part of the house he needed them. And they never, ever, went into the basement. Only invited guests went there, sometimes to see his artificial wine cellar, other times to see his one-of-a-kind gaming room with whatever latest computer equipment he'd read about. Victor Someone was into miniature train sets, of all the ridiculous things, and to his delight he discovered that D was, too! In fact, D had what some considered the most elaborate miniature train setup east of the Mississippi and wouldn't Victor like to see that? Why yes, yes he would. It's right down here, in the basement, please come, I'll show you. D had shown him, and like all the guests invited into D's basement, Victor Someone had not come back alive.

He was bored with Victor already. He'd stared at the idiot's driver's license for part of the morning, trying to relive the excitement of the kill, but there had been so little then or now. It was like trying to remember the marvelous taste of an especially bland meal. He gave up after his first cup of tea and half his muffin, tossed the driver's license aside and focused on the two dozen responses he'd gotten from his ad on ManMate. He'd worded it carefully to hint at his wealth and age without coming right out and presenting himself as a sugar daddy. He preferred ones with some intelligence, not run-of-the-mill hustlers. The more success they had in the world, the more they were able to hold an interesting conversation, the more he enjoyed their company for a short while before inviting them to see whatever he'd determined they wanted to see in his basement. He extracted just enough information from them to fantasize something down there they would want to see, and it always worked. But the dumb ones, the hustlers and the rent boys? They were only there for one thing, quick and easy. D was not interested in killing men no one would miss. He wanted worthy prey, so he placed his ads to attract it:

Single older man seeks friendship and possible traveling companion. Enjoy fine dining, theater, quality wine and quality time. Not looking for hookups or one-night stands. You should be intelligent, engaging, fully self-supporting and interested in seeing the city and possibly the world with your new best friend. Must be over 30 and easy on the eyes. Photo with all replies please.

It was broad yet specific enough to get at least some responses from the types of men he was looking for. Victor had been an anomaly, a customer he'd never seen before but whose amazing blue eyes and easy smile had tripped him up, caught him off guard. He did not make mistakes, and would not make one again. He'd paid for it in a lackluster kill that left him unsatisfied. He planned to make up for it with the next one.

There were sixteen responses to his ad. Eight of them he immediately deleted; four he pondered, scanning their photographs with his eyes to see if what initially caught his fancy lasted more then a few moments. It didn't, so he deleted those as well. That left four more. One was African-American and quite handsome. He'd sent a photograph of himself in dress military uniform. D had no idea what branch of service it was, but clearly this man was a serious candidate. D minimized the photograph and moved to the next one. This gentleman—for someone clearly in his 50s ought to be called a gentleman—was also very handsome and well-groomed, salt-and-pepper buzz cut, no glasses, although D suspected he wore them, at least for reading. He was a keeper, so D saved his email and photo. The last two were younger, one Asian, one white. D did not consider himself a racist or especially biased (not to be confused with discerning, which he most certainly was), but Asians were never really his cup of tea. As attractive as the man was, in a suit and tie, no less, he didn't fit the bill. D deleted him, leaving him with three choices.

Decisions, decisions. The fourth and final applicant was very good looking indeed. Dressed casually, "Kevin," as he called himself, listed his age as 32 and his occupation as branch manager for one of the largest bank chains in the city. Kevin lived in Staten Island—a very long way to travel to meet someone from an online ad, but that could be advantageous for D. The further away from home his victim came, the farther afield the police would have to search (futilely, he might add). Kevin had a disarming smile, sparkling brown eyes, longish sandy hair and a button-down shirt, the sort a bank manager might wear on his off-time.

In the end D said goodbye to the military man. He was truly appealing, but also too great a risk. Someone who had served his country might be very quick in a struggle. D had to consider his own strength and age. He could not take a chance at losing the upper hand; and while he drugged his victims first, it was just enough to make them woozy. The kill was a disappointment if they were incapacitated. He'd learned that early on when he first started. An unconscious man was no more interesting than a dead one. No, he would have to pass on Mr. Military, musing on how lucky the man was without ever knowing it.

That left Kevin the bank manager and Scott the well-preserved 50-something. Scott gave no indication what he did for a living or where he lived. If D wanted to know more he would have to respond. Did he want to know more? He peered closely at Scott's picture. Damn, he was a nice looking man. Not too tall, either. D didn't like taller men.

Suddenly D found himself in a unique situation. He had always been able to narrow it down to one. On occasion that one proved to be a poor choice and he'd had to start over, but it had always been one at a time. Now he could not decide.

He took another bite of his muffin and felt his frustration rise—and his curiosity. What was going on with him? His first kill had been uninspiring, even uneventful. And now he could not make a decision! Was it because the two remaining candidates were so different—one older than D, one younger? One vague in his email, saying little about himself, the other an eager bank branch manager whose email, short at it was, seemed written to let D know he was "fully self-supporting" and mature for his age?

Damn, D thought, sliding his plate to the side. *Damn, damn, damn.* This was not like him. This was indecisive. This was ... thrilling in its way. Maybe he needed to switch things up. Yes, maybe that was the lesson of Victor Someone. It wasn't that he'd been away from it too long, wasting three years in a dreary German city, unable to speak the language well at first and tending to his pathetic mother out of a sense of obligation that had surprised him after all these years. It wasn't that he'd lost his passion. It was simply that he needed some spice, some new twists. Meeting two men instead of one would certainly be that. He always met them first. In his initial meetings he said nothing of who he was or where he worked, the men's clothing store he owned or where he lived. He was simply a well-heeled, well-mannered man from a city teeming with them, and they were unsuspecting prey.

He would do it! He would respond to each of them and set a time with Kevin for a casual coffee at the Arlington, perhaps meet Scott in a discreet bar. He hated chain coffee shops; nothing could be more banal than meeting in a Starbucks. But the Arlington served coffee and tea in their lobby. The landmark hotel had changed a great deal. The ghosts of celebrities from the 1930s and 40s had been chased away by tourists from Idaho and South Dakota. But the place still had atmosphere and the illusion of something once grand. It was one of his meeting places, but not the only one. He had to be careful; hotel clerks, servers and baristas had memories and could give descriptions. There were cameras absolutely everywhere, too. Most times D would meet them in a park—Bryant Park, or even the majestic Central Park—but not always. Sometimes a public meeting with witnesses added a touch of danger. He felt like being dangerous. He would not have the second one be as boring as the first.

He took a deep breath and felt an involuntary smile spread across his face. He placed his fingers over the laptop keyboard, then began thinking of his reply to each man. Wording was key. He would meet them each, one late morning and one in the afternoon. Jarrod would mind the store. He'd minded it for three years and done a very commendable job. It's why D had hired him; he knew a quality man when he saw one. And now he was looking at two!

He began to type.

5

Kyle was determined their visit with Detective Linda would be different this time. On her last trip they'd been consumed by their search for the killer Kieran Stipling—whose name and motive they didn't know until they'd stopped his killing spree on a SoHo rooftop. There had been no time to see the city, no time to stroll or stop at one of the coffee shops on every other corner; no time to visit Grand Central terminal and gaze in awe at the ceiling with its constellations or marvel at the human river flowing in, out and around the magnificent train station every day. This time Kyle would show her the city he'd loved since moving here fresh out of college with his then-boyfriend David. He realized, as they walked west on 23rd Street, that it had been over thirty years since then. The city had changed. He had changed. The world itself was a very different place.

"Welcome to Chelsea," Kyle said as they crossed Sixth Avenue. "Once a gay mecca, now more a blend of strollers and gays and yuppies—does anyone still say 'yuppie'?"

Linda was taking it all in. Her memories of New York City were not the best: she'd stayed away from the city for many years, not wanting to taint the memory of her trip here as a child just months before her father was killed in Cincinnati; then, when she finally returned last year, she was pursuing a murderer not long after stepping off a train at Penn Station. Kyle's photography exhibit opening at the Katherine

Pride Gallery had been wonderful, but the next day she was gone again. She could not yet say what she thought of the city, not really.

"Why do they call it Chelsea?" she asked. The only other Chelsea she knew of was in London. She also knew it was the kind of information Kyle would have; he was a sponge for just this sort of trivia.

It was warm out, but not yet humid. Kyle hated the humidity that came with summers in Manhattan. It was the only season he didn't like, and he knew come July he would have his annual impulse to move to Seattle or San Francisco, places he'd never been but that he imagined remained in the cool 70s all year round. He wouldn't move, of course, but he would want to.

"Funny you should ask," Kyle said. "It was originally an estate of a British major, who called it Chelsea in honor of Sir Thomas Moore's estate in London. Land was added to it over the years and it became the Chelsea we're walking in. Which, by the way, mysteriously expanded since I moved here."

"Really?"

"Yes. Chelsea twenty years ago ran from 14th Street to 23rd. They extended it to 34th Street when the neighborhood gentrified so they could attract renters. Funny how that works. North of 34th it's Hell's Kitchen, which was called Clinton for awhile, but now that there's nothing the least bit seedy or dangerous about it everybody calls it Hell's Kitchen again. It gives the residents someplace interesting to say they live."

They were both wearing shorts today, a rarity for Kyle who preferred his legs covered in public, and he was thankful Linda would have perfect weather for her brief visit with them. She was leaving for Phoenix on Monday and he wanted her to have a good time, something to take her mind off the situation with her terminally ill mother-in-law.

"I'm sorry about Kirsten's mother," he said.

"Dot. That's what everybody calls her, she'd tell you to call her that, too."

"Dot."

"I like that name. Dorothy's nice, but there's something unique about Dot. I don't know any other Dots, do you?"

"I can't say I do," Kyle said.

"It's hard. But Kirsten's holding up through it. She has to. I can't tell you how much it meant to her for Dot to make it one last time to New Jersey for our wedding. And how much it meant to me that you and Danny were there."

They were nearing Eighth Avenue now and Linda noticed several couples holding hands. Men with men, and at least one young lesbian couple who seemed happy and in love as they stopped to look at puppies in a pet shop window. A sadness came over her as she thought of all the years she'd missed, all the years she had kept her truest self a secret. At the same time, she was thrilled to live in a changing world, a world in which she could walk down the street—at least some streets, in some cities—holding Kirsten's hand without succumbing to the impulse to hide.

"Where are we going?" Linda asked. Kyle had told her he wanted to take a walk, but not where they were walking to. Danny had gone to his restaurant to meet with Chloe the day manager, and to plan for what would be both a celebration and the saddest event of his life: saying goodbye to old Margaret Bowman as she prepared to move to Florida. Danny was the party planner, as he had been for every party at Margaret's Passion the last eleven years. Kyle had suggested Danny let someone else arrange this one, that it would be too difficult, but Danny would have none of it. It was his restaurant, purchased from Margaret, and she was his second mother. No, he'd said, this was something he had to do.

"I want you to meet Imogene," Kyle said as they kept walking west. Once they reached Ninth Avenue they would turn right and head toward 38th Street. It was a good long walk, and he planned to stop for coffee and bagels as he always did, taking one of each for his boss, Imogene Landis. He wondered briefly if she, too, would be moving on soon. It was not a welcome thought and he waved it aside.

"Bugs?" Linda said, seeing Kyle wave his hand in the air.

"No, just something I don't want to think about."

Imogene Landis was a television reporter who'd slid very near the bottom of her profession until events gave her career a second wind. When Kyle started working as her assistant six years ago she'd been reduced to a position as the English language financial reporter for a show called Tokyo Pulse. The show was put out by Japan TV3, whose studios they were walking toward. The 3:00 a.m. Tokyo crowd got a good laugh out of Imogene; she knew nothing about financial reporting, and her attempts to include a few words in Japanese had them howling on their living rooms floors. Then, a year and a half ago, she'd covered the murders at Pride Lodge—the same murders that brought Kyle and Linda together, and the next thing she knew, she was a star. A minor star, to be sure, but bright enough for her bosses in Tokyo and the New York station manager, Leonard Baumstein ("Lenny-san"), to promote her to city reporter. Since then she'd been back in the thick of things, covering politics, art, even the occasional noteworthy homicide. She was a celebrity of sorts now, and she'd caught the eye of several TV stations across the country. Kyle believed it was only a matter of time before one of them made her an offer she would accept.

They reached Ninth Avenue and turned, walking north. Most of New York City was a grid, something Kyle appreciated. It was both easy to find your way here, and harder to get lost. He'd walked this way a thousand times and wondered if he would keep walking this way if there was no Imogene waiting. He supposed he would, as a matter of habit, at least for awhile.

"I haven't wanted to bring this up ..." he said

Linda knew he was talking about the news he'd read that morning.

"There's nothing you can do, Kyle. Maybe it's not who you think it is, this Pride Killer. Maybe your doorman's brother drowned in the river. People drink too much, sometimes they stumble."

"No, this wasn't an accident. It's him. I know it is."

"So leave it to the police."

"You *are* the police!"

"Retired, Kyle. And I was on the New Hope force, a long way and a world of difference from New York City. I have a bad feeling about this one, I think we should stay out of it."

"And wait to read about two more? He kills in threes. No, this time he struck close to home. This time it's personal. I want to talk to Vinnie."

"Your doorman?"

"Yes, when the time's right." Kyle didn't know when Vincent Campagna would return to work but when he did, Kyle wanted to have a very delicate conversation with him.

"Well," said Linda, "if this is the Pride Killer and he claims his victims every Pride weekend –"

"Minus the last two."

"Minus the last two ... I'd say time isn't something we have much of."

She was right. Kyle sighed, knowing he ought to stay out of it, but what if this killer got away with it again? He'd done his dirty work for years before stopping, and now that he was back he would probably do it for years again. Something had to be done, but not this moment. For now Kyle was taking them to meet his beloved, infuriating, demanding boss, and that was where his mind should be.

"Cecil's is just up ahead," Kyle said. Cecil's was the bagel shop where he always bought coffee and a breakfast treat of some kind for himself and Imogene. He was comforted that Cecil's had been around as long as it had—at least as long as Kyle had worked for Imogene. Some things needed to stay the same, he thought, even if it's just a bagel shop. Otherwise the impermanence of life would be too much to bear.

"I could use another cup of coffee," Linda said.

They walked on, approaching the back of the Port Authority bus terminal. Some parts of New York City were breathtaking, and other parts were permanently ugly. But this is New York City, all of it, and Kyle wanted Linda to see as much of it as she could in the next four days. He put the thought of killers and floating bodies out of his mind for now. It was a glorious day at one of the most festive times of year, at least for the hundreds of thousands who would flood Fifth Avenue for the parade Sunday, and he wanted no rain, no sadness, no death. This morning he would have none of them.

6

Keller and Whitman was not the most well known men's clothing store in Manhattan, but it was certainly considered among the best. D's uncle, Leo Whitman, had eschewed growth, turning his nose up at the bigger stores and having disdain for chain operations. He was interested in quality, not quantity, and he had educated D slowly and steadily in the ways of the discerning man. *You succeeded very well, Uncle,* D thought as he entered the store that bore his name. *Not only are my customers discerning, but I'm quite the connoisseur myself. Take Kevin, for instance ...*

He was in especially good spirits this morning. The letdown of his first kill had eased and he attributed it to being out of practice. His time in Berlin had numbed his senses, like eating too much bad food for too long, then suddenly tasting something exquisite. His palate had not been ready for it, but it would be the next time. He was back in form.

"Good morning, Mr. K," Jarrod said when he saw D come through the front door.

Jarrod Sperling was a good man and an even better store manager. His efficiency and way with customers, each of whom he made to feel as if they were the only truly valuable customer in the world, were what had saved him from becoming D's third victim nearly seven years ago. Had it not been for these qualities D spotted in him when they met for a drink, Jarrod would be a forgotten headline now. But he'd impressed D with his manners and his knowledge of the garment business, and instead of killing him D hired him to help with the store. In very quick order Jarrod proved himself capable of keeping things going on his own, and he'd run the business very well when D was in Berlin. For that D must find a way to thank him. Perhaps a ridiculously large Christmas bonus.

"Good morning, Jarrod. I trust you're well."

"Very, Mr. K. And I have good news."

I have even better news, D thought, *but I'll never be able to tell you.*

"What might that be?"

"You know Michael Marzen …"

"I know *of* Michael Marzen, yes. He's on the cover of everything these days."

Michael Marzen was a software billionaire who had decided to gift most of his fortune to charity. Charities, of course, had lined up for a piece of the action, and Marzen had been giving interviews on the virtues of philanthropy.

"Well," said Jarrod, in a deliberately self-effacing way, bowing his head just so as if to say he was a humble man, with humble tidings, "He wants a new wardrobe, and he wants it from Keller and Whitman."

This was indeed good news. A man of Marzen's means could provide the store with enough income to show a profit for the year. Keller and Whitman always showed a profit, but this would be exceptional.

"Good man," D said.

Jarrod blushed and smiled, not quite a puppy who'd been patted on the head, but almost.

"Now how about a cup of tea from the bakery? And get a scone for yourself, something to tide you over. I'll be taking lunch out today. I have a prospective client to meet. Not nearly as wealthy or famous as Michael Marzen, but a true catch … if I'm able to catch him."

"Oh my," Jarrod said. "You haven't lost your touch, Mr. K."

"No, I haven't."

Jarrod then did as he was told and left the store, walking briskly across Lexington Avenue to the small bakery that had served the Upper East Side neighborhood for twenty years. They were top notch, with a reputation that needed no preceding, and had been satisfying the tastes of fickle customers since they first opened their doors. D would skip the scones. He never ate before an interview.

Deidrich Kristof Keller III moved to New York City—Brooklyn, to be precise—when his mother went crawling back to Germany in defeat. He was only sixteen at the time, living in the wasteland that was Anaheim, California. It had Disneyland, but that only served to make the point. Even as a teenager, D saw humanity as a vast sea of half-awake people stumbling through their lives from one event to the next, with the in-between filled by boredom. Anaheim was utterly boring. He hated it, and wondered why his parents ever moved there.

His father, also Deidrich, amounted to little and was so unimaginative that he'd thought a large, dull swath of land in Southern California was the place to be. He took his then-pregnant wife and moved from Germany to America, imagining himself an adventurer. But he was not; the most adventurous thing he ever did was also the thing that made D hate him so much—he left his wife and son when D was twelve. Not only did he leave them to fend for themselves in a land both of them despised (D's mother never did like this strange country with its over-inflated sense of itself), but he left them for a man! D's father, it turned out, was running not just from a life he found lacking, but to a life he fantasized silently about until one day he announced at breakfast that he was leaving. He did not say where he was going, or whom he planned to meet there, but D and his mother knew. Samuel was the man's name. He met D's father at the Boeing factory in Anaheim where both men worked assembling aircraft. For a year the two men spent all their spare time together and Marta Keller, while pretending there was nothing amiss as Samuel became a fourth member of their family, knew better. Her husband had changed. He had become happy. He had never been happy with her, and he always treated his son as a peculiar child he wanted nothing to do with but felt obligated to raise.

That sense of obligation vanished one Saturday morning. D was eating pancakes at their small kitchen table. Marta was making a second stack for her husband, with several sausages in a small skillet next to the pancakes, when D's father walked into the room carrying a duffel bag. He announced he was moving to San Francisco with Samuel, picked a sausage from the skillet, bit half and tossed the rest back with the others, and left. Just like that. D never spoke to the man again.

Marta Keller tried to hang on. She got an office job at the same Boeing factory where her traitorous husband met the man of his dreams and her nightmares. She worked there for four years, slowly descending into the neurotic depressed woman she would spend the rest of her life being. Finally, as abruptly as Deidrich Keller had left his family, she told D they were moving back to Germany. As much as he hated Anaheim, he knew nothing of Berlin. He didn't speak the language, and imagined Germany to be a cold wet country cloaked in guilt and regret for its crimes against humanity. He resisted. He was sixteen by then and all but self-sufficient. Marta at last gave him an option (though running away had become his first choice, had things not taken a turn for the better): he could go to Berlin with her, or he could move to Brooklyn and live with his uncle Leo. Leo Whitman was her older brother and had moved to the United States a decade before the Kellers moved to California. Leo was also a successful tailor, unmarried, and willing to take his nephew in. D had only met the man once, when Leo came to visit during Christmas. D was ten years old. The Kellers never went to Brooklyn and D had no idea what it was like, but he believed it must be more interesting than where he was. Any place would be. He jumped at the chance, acted as if it were a difficult choice, and said goodbye to his mother one rainy September. By the evening of that day he was living in Brooklyn, set on a path that changed his life completely, and his mother was on an overnight flight to Berlin.

It was D's idea to open a store on the Upper East Side, D's cajoling and flattering that got his uncle Leo to believe he could be more than a very fine tailor for a very fine clientele. It was also D's money, earned and saved from a series of side jobs while he helped his uncle grow his business, that got them started. Hence the name Keller and Whitman. D played his cards carefully and never suggested he was more than an eager apprentice learning at the knee of a master, but when it came time to open the store he insisted, in the nicest way one can insist, that his name come first. Leo Whitman had no objections, and when D was twenty-two he became a businessman. Ten years later he was a *very successful* businessman, clothier to celebrities and politicians. A year after that he bought his townhouse, thanked his uncle for everything he'd made possible for D, then shoved him down the stairs of the five-flight walkup they shared. D told the police it was a tragedy waiting to happen. Leo was in frail health, he said, and D had tried to convince him for years to move to an elevator building. Leo would have none of it, and one day D came home from work to find his uncle with a broken neck at the bottom of the stairs. It had all been terribly sad. He'd cried and cried but carried on in his uncle's memory. Marta Keller did not come for the funeral. D inherited everything.

D enjoyed his tea while Jarrod nibbled at his blueberry scone in the back office. Food was not allowed in the store, and only D was allowed to have a beverage in front. He kept it below the cash register where he could quickly conceal it if a customer came in. It was just eleven o'clock and only two men had come to the store, one a regular client and the other looking for a suit for a funeral. D had attended to them both and already made two sales for the day.

Jarrod came back in, having carefully wiped his hands and any stray crumbs from his sport coat. Jarrod had just turned fifty-three and was, to D's knowledge, eternally single. His fastidiousness might be the cause, D thought, but it made Jarrod a very good store manager.

"I'm leaving now, Jarrod," D said, finishing his tea and handing his trusted manager the cup.

"Anyone I might know?" Jarrod asked. He rarely asked questions, but there had always been a nosiness to him when it came to clients. Even a man who had checked the inseams of some of New York City's most powerful and influential players could still be star struck.

"No one I might know of, either!" D said, with a short practiced laugh. "No, just someone who was referred to me and is staying at the Arlington. I've arranged to meet him for coffee.

D was just about to leave the store when Jarrod said, "Did you see the news this morning?"

D stopped halfway to the door. He knew he'd made a mistake giving into his impulse with Victor, but he knew, too, that Jarrod would never connect his boss with what happened.

"I'm afraid I did not," D said.

"A young man was found dead in the East River early Tuesday morning."

"Really?"

"Yes, and there was something very familiar about him. They showed his picture on the news. I'd swear he was here the other day."

D, his back to Jarrod, said, "He may have been. We get so much traffic some days, Jarrod, I can't remember everyone who walks in the door."

Jarrod thought a moment, trying to remember. "Victor, they said. That was his name. Victor something."

"Victor something." D's voice was flat and emotionless. "That's quite an unusual name. Now I really must be going. I leave the store in your capable hands, as always."

"As always!"

The compliment worked, distracting Jarrod's attention away from the news and a man he vaguely remembered seeing in the store.

"Memory plays tricks on us all, Jarrod. I'd think nothing of it."

"No, Sir, I won't. Good luck with the new client."

"Luck has nothing to do with it." D glanced at his reflection in the store window and walked out onto Lexington Avenue. June had brought the first real warmth of the season. For a moment he held his face up to the sky, appreciating the sun and the clearness of the day, then he began walking west.

7

The television studio for Japan TV3 was originally a garment factory, an outlier in what was once a thriving industry in New York City. Fifty years ago, and for many preceding decades, fabrics were central to Manhattan's industrial machine. Long contained in an area called the garment district that stretches from Sixth to Ninth Avenues east-to-west and between 34th and 40th Streets south-to-north, it still serves as a center of fashion, with some of the world's leading designers maintaining factories, but the days of clothing the world are long gone. Shirts, dresses and all other kinds of clothes are now made for a few dollars by people earning pennies in places like Indonesia, Thailand and Bangladesh. But when "Made in America" was the norm, the factory that now housed a Japanese-owned television studio and its offices was humming with the sounds of sewing machines and the silence of an army of workers whose job was to sew, not talk.

Kyle explained all this to Linda as they walked the last few blocks along Ninth Avenue and turned left at 38th, heading west another long block. Linda was impressed if not quite dazzled by the sheer number of people in this city. She also noticed, as Kyle had when he first moved here, the tendency people had to move quickly for no apparent reason. They seemed to maneuver more than walk, each wanting an advantage over the rest in terms of how quickly they got where they were going.

"Why's everyone in such a hurry?" Linda asked as they reached the studio.

"Because they think they have to be," Kyle said. "You can sense it the moment you get back into Manhattan from anywhere, this rush everyone's in."

"And they do it all without seeing where they're going!" She was referring to the omnipresence of smartphones, headsets and ear buds. Almost everyone had one, their eyes fixed on tiny screens in their hands, their ears plugged and deadened by music, their thumbs twitching out text messages and emails. They had all this in rural New Jersey, too, but it was decidedly slower there. Even New Hope, which was as big-city as it got around the area where Linda lived, wasn't nearly as visibly distracted and manic as this.

Kyle held the door for Linda and followed her into the studio. It was like many buildings in this part of the city, architecturally interesting on the outside, with its century-old brickwork and large windows, but basically a series of boxes on the inside. The exception was the second floor studio, which had been divided into three units where programs were made for a mostly-Tokyo audience. The offices where Kyle worked were on the third floor, with the first floor given to nondescript and unidentified rooms.

"What's on the first floor?" Linda asked.

"I have no idea," Kyle replied. "You can spend years in a building here and not know who your neighbors are." He waved at Franklin, the security guard by the front door who had never been required to secure anything and whose waking state only appeared different from his sleeping state because his eyes were open.

Kyle led them past the elevator to the stairs and opened the stairwell door.

"Aren't we taking the elevator?" Linda asked.

"It's broken."

"For how long?"

"Oh, about six months. Don't worry, you won't be winded. It's only two flights up."

Kyle walked up the stairs carrying a bag with coffee and a bagel for Imogene, and a cup of fruit for their station manager, Lenny-san. He was Jewish but everyone called him that because the bosses in Tokyo did. Kyle, however, had never been Kyle-san.

They reached the third floor and Kyle opened the door, ushering Linda onto a brightly lit floor that looked like a million others in offices everywhere. It was an open seating plan, with a maze of cubicles. Only Lenny-san had an office. Linda followed along as Kyle headed down one row of cubes, turned left at the far wall and walked down another row identical to the one they'd just passed. Finally, in the southwest corner, he reached the cubicle he'd spent his workdays in for the last six years. Next to it, unmistakably, was Imogene Landis's. She had installed tall plants at the entrance to her cube and strung a row of blinking lights. Had she not been one of the stars of the operation none of this would be tolerated and Imogene would surely have left, even if it meant stringing her lights and watering her plants at home while she collected unemployment.

"Oh! My! God!" Imogene shouted when she saw him. "You're on vacation, Kyle, what the fuck are you doing here?" Imogene was known for her loudness and her inappropriate language. "Don't tell me you came here to bring me coffee and a bagel!"

Linda noticed that Imogene tended to exclaim everything.

"Oh, wait, of course!" Imogene said, jumping up out of her chair. "You came to introduce me to … to …"

"Detective Linda," Kyle said. Linda was retired but had stopped correcting him months ago.

"Detective Linda," Imogene said, putting her hand out. "*The* Detective Linda. You solved the Pride Lodge murders."

Linda demurred. "Well, yes and no. I investigated them."

"That's right, that's right. The killer got away."

"One of them," Kyle said. "But we're not here to talk about that. I wanted to show Linda where I worked, and to introduce you."

Imogene Landis was diminutive and thin, a pixie of a woman with an outsized voice and an even bigger personality. She was wearing red cat-eyes glasses attached to a black necklace around her neck. When she was in front of the camera or out in public—anywhere but the office and at home—the glasses came off. She would prefer to see the world through blurred vision than have the world know she needed corrective lenses.

"Where's Lenny-san?" Kyle asked, looking at the empty office with its lights off. "I brought him some fruit."

Lenny-san had been on a diet for several years, the length of it extended because he would have his fruit and top it off with a chocolate croissant he'd snuck in in his briefcase.

"I can't say," Imogene said. "He doesn't tell me when he's coming in late. He'll be here. Just leave the fruit with me, unless you plan on staying awhile."

"No," said Kyle. "Just a few minutes. It is my vacation day and I'd rather not get roped into anything."

"I'd love to get roped into something," Imogene said. She was always looking out for the next big story. The Pride Lodge murders were fading into memory and she needed something explosive. "What have you heard?"

"Nothing," Kyle said. He was concerned about being waylaid and was already thinking they shouldn't have come. He was a loyal assistant, but that came with a cost. Imogene emailed him and called him at all hours, and as often as she'd promised not to, she still did it out of habit.

"There was a news item this morning," Linda said.

Kyle shot her a glance and Linda realized her mistake.

"What news item was that?" Imogene took her coffee and bagel from Kyle and set it on her desk.

"Nothing."

She looked at him like a cat eyeing a toy. "Come on, Kyle, you know something."

"I don't know anything. It was just a body found in the river."

"Oooooh, I like that."

Imogene was not heartless, she was simply driven. She knew dead bodies did not get their feelings hurt, so she kept it honest. Dead bodies in rivers were interesting, depending on how they got there.

"Fine," Kyle said. "But it's your story to run with. I'm not working on it with you, I'm not calling sources, I wasn't even here this morning. You're imagining me."

"Deal. Just some details, that's all, I'll take it from there."

"Well," Kyle said, "I don't know if you remember the Pride Killer."

"Of course I do. He killed people every Gay Weekend or something."

"Pride weekend. It's not called 'Gay Weekend.'"

"Am I not supposed to say 'gay' anymore? I can't keep up with the language, it all becomes offensive to someone so quickly."

Kyle sighed. Imogene was hopeless in some ways, amazing in others. He looked at Linda, who had decided to lean against the outer cubicle wall and watch it all with amusement.

"The Pride Killer did his killing for three or four years in June every year, coinciding with the Pride festivities. Yes, they're gay. They're a lot of other things too, including the time of year he terrorized the gay community. Then, three years ago, he stopped. He was never caught, obviously. The police never even had any suspects, unless they kept that to themselves. We thought he'd died or gone to prison for something else, or simply moved away. But a body was found in the East River early Tuesday morning and I'm convinced he's back."

"Good, good," Imogene said. She had grabbed a reporter's notebook and pen and was quickly jotting things down in her own indecipherable scribble. "Not good that someone's dead, of course, but the good start to a story. What else do you know?"

"Nothing."

"You're lying."

Goddamn her, Kyle thought. Maybe getting this close to anyone was a mistake. Only Danny could read him that easily and quickly.

"Okay," Kyle said. "So the young man he killed was the brother of our doorman."

"Can you get me an interview?"

"No! You're out of your mind. For one thing, he's been on leave the past two nights, for obvious reasons. For another … no … you can't interview him. At least not through me."

"So give me a name."

Kyle thought about it a moment. Imogene was a relentless newshound and would put it together soon enough once she read the item in that day's New York Times.

"Vincent Campagna," he said. "He's our overnight doorman. His brother was Victor."

"The dead guy."

"The victim," Kyle reminded her. "Don't forget that. And if you follow up on this, you can say nothing about where you got this information. You read it in the paper, you spoke to the police. I had nothing to do with it."

"Fine," Imogene said. "It's nothing I can't find out from other sources, but it expedites things."

Kyle realized that Linda had been standing there saying nothing for ten minutes. He'd intended for the two women to have more of an introduction, but after spilling the beans to Imogene he decided it was best to leave.

"We're heading to breakfast," Kyle said. He wanted out of the office and food was always a good excuse.

"It was so nice to meet you," Imogene said to Linda. They'd met at Kyle's photography exhibit but had only spoken for a moment. Imogene was there covering it for Tokyo Pulse, a gift to Kyle he had neither asked for nor wanted.

"Likewise," Linda said. She'd taken what measure she could of Kyle's boss and would think it through later. She sensed she and Imogene would either be friends or, just as likely, not like each other beyond a certain civility. Imogene was New York City in a five-foot-one frame and Linda wasn't sure she could take the woman for more than a few minutes.

As they were about to leave, Kyle said, "One thing, Imogene …"

"Yes?"

He spoke with all seriousness. "This one's truly nasty."

Imogene smiled. "I wasn't planning on interviewing the killer, unless he's in a jail cell."

"I'm serious. He's cold and cruel and not someone you should go anywhere near. If you happen to get any ideas about his identity, call the cops. He's gotten away with a dozen murders and he won't hesitate to make you one more."

"I can handle myself," she said.

"I imagine that's what all the men he's killed thought, too. Now goodbye. I'll see you Monday. After 'Gay Weekend.'"

"Get outta here! And take this wonderful Amazonian with you. So nice to meet you!"

"You're repeating yourself," Kyle said. "I'll see you next week. And put Lenny-san's fruit cup in the refrigerator before it ferments."

Kyle waved a last time and led Linda back along the cubicles the way they'd come. As they walked down the stairs, he thought of the warning he'd given Imogene and how he and Detective Linda ought to heed it themselves. This killer was different. This killer was meticulous—he had to be to get away with it for so long. This killer did not make mistakes, or so the man thought. Everyone makes mistakes, and as Kyle and Linda exited back onto 38th Street, Kyle knew it was the mistakes he had to look for—very, very carefully.

8

Danny arrived at Margaret's Passion ten minutes after leaving the apartment. It was one of the perks of working there—he had been able to walk to work and home for over a decade. And while he loved being so close to the restaurant he now called his, he had also been close to Margaret Bowman all this time, and that very long chapter in his life was coming to a close. Margaret, as strong and determined as she had been for eighty-two years, was about to move to Florida. Danny had known for several years this was inevitable but he'd kept putting it out of his mind, just as Margaret had kept putting off her decision to move. The time had finally come; the arrangements had been made, and now all that was left was to celebrate Margaret's life and achievements and say goodbye. He did not know if he would see her again. He knew if he did, it would mean taking a trip to Florida—she was not coming back to New York City. Danny had never been to Florida and believed he would die having never enjoyed its stifling humidity, vast flatness, and throngs of the elderly. But for Margaret he would go. At her age, in her health, it meant a trip that wouldn't be put off too long, either.

Margaret's Passion had been in business for over thirty years. It started as a dream Margaret had when she worked for her parents' small Italian restaurant in what was then Little Italy. It was still called that, but there was almost nothing Italian left about it. Chinatown had muscled in long ago, and the Italians had moved on, mostly out of Manhattan to the outer boroughs (as had just about everyone who wasn't wealthy enough to live on the millionaire's row the City had become). Now it was a figment of the tourist imagination. Margaret had been prescient, and also not interested in labeling her restaurant with a specific ethnicity. She and her husband Gerard, so young then, started their restaurant near Gramercy Park, and there it remained. They eventually bought the building the restaurant was in; it occupied the first floor, with three floors of tenants above it. The Bowmans themselves lived on the second floor, with a connecting staircase they'd installed (without city permits, but no one's telling) that ran down into the kitchen of the restaurant. It was how they came up and down without leaving the building.

Margaret had been taking those stairs to visit her guests for three decades—and she meant it sincerely, knowing them by name, knowing their children's birthdays and the major events in their lives; this was no "Next guest!" you hear now being shouted by drug store clerks who couldn't care less if you were a guest or a corpse. Margaret loved and was beloved.

Time took its toll, and eventually Margaret stopped coming down to the restaurant. Then, as things came full circle, Danny made the trip up the stairs to see her. Her Danny, her adopted son. She and Gerard had no children. Then Gerard was struck and killed by a taxi not ten feet from the building. Danny never met Gerard Bowman, but he knew Margaret loved the man with whom she had done it all. He knew she loved *him*, too. She was Danny's second mother, something he did not say out loud to his own mother in Astoria. But everybody knew how much they meant to each other, and how hard this was going to be.

It had fallen on Danny to arrange the going away party for Margaret. The planning had gone on for several months now. Danny worked closely with Chloe, the new day manager. That had been Danny's job until he bought the restaurant with Kyle and Kyle's mother. (If it had been Kyle's mother's *money* he would be much happier, but Sally Callahan insisted on being part of the package.) Danny had been planning the restaurant's events for a long time. Several private parties a year were held there, by the types of people who arrived in motorcades and were sometimes preceded by security details. Among the most star-studded events he'd organized was Margaret Bowman's eighty-first birthday a little over a year ago. He wondered if it had been some kind of signal for Margaret, telling her the time to leave was getting near; or a dress rehearsal for what he was planning now. So many big-name politicians, entertainment figures and philanthropists had shown up that Danny had made the decision to hold a separate, private birthday party with the staff and a few true intimates, including himself. He had worked the main party but had not taken up one of the highly valued sixty seats the restaurant was limited to. Margaret wasn't happy about it, either, but she knew they could not risk excluding someone whose name was on a Broadway marquee or a ballot in the next election. She wanted them all to keep coming there when she was gone, so she had acquiesced; in the end she had a much better time with just her staff, Danny, Kyle, and a half dozen people who could say they truly knew her.

This event was different. It was the last Margaret would attend, and it was her going away celebration. Danny had even wondered if they should have it somewhere else with twice the seating capacity. But that would be wrong and everyone there would know it. This was a party to say goodbye to Margaret, and it could only be held in her restaurant. Memories could not be packed up and transported to another location.

Chloe was waiting for him when he got there. The restaurant didn't open until 11:30 a.m. (only lunch and dinner were served at Margaret's Passion), but there was always a lot of preparation, and Chloe had proved to be as meticulous in her job as Danny had been when it was his. She had been with the restaurant for five years, working as a lunch server, bar back, you-name-it. Chloe was Danny's right hand, and he was glad to offer her his job when he became the owner. No one else had even been considered.

"You really should have taken some days off," Chloe said when Danny arrived. He knew she'd already been there for at least an hour, doing Chloe things, which often extended to jobs well below her pay grade. Nothing was beneath Chloe, and that's one of the things Danny liked about her.

Chloe was tall and thin and sometimes mistaken for a man. She had very short hair and a flat chest she was neither proud nor ashamed of. Her mother was in a nursing home with early-onset Alzheimer's (Chloe was only thirty-six). That was all Danny knew of her personal life. He didn't even know if she was straight, gay, bi, trans, or none of the above. She was a phenomenal asset to the restaurant, a good person who loved the old woman who lived upstairs almost as much as Danny did, and that was all he wanted to know.

"I can't take time off right now, Chloe," Danny said. "Too much to do."

"But your detective friend is here, that seems important."

Danny thought of telling her that Linda was really Kyle's friend. He considered her his friend, too, but not in the best-friends-forever category. He also sometimes felt like a third wheel when they were together, and he was content letting Kyle take Linda around the City. Besides, he had a party to plan—the saddest, least-wanted party he would ever throw, and it was time to get down to business.

"Come," Danny said, sitting at a table and waving Chloe over. "We have names to cross out."

As with Margaret's birthday party, this one involved starting with a list almost twice the size of its final draft, then eliminating names after painstakingly discussing who should not be on it, and whom they could afford to offend. Luckily, the new mayor was scheduled to be out of town (Margaret didn't much care for the man's politics). The previous mayor, on the other hand, would have to be accommodated.

Danny sighed. Dealing with egos was part of his job and it had only gotten harder since he was now the owner. Favors were expected, and although Margaret had always maintained a strict egalitarian approach to seating (reservations were a must, and could not be bought at the expense of a customer who already had a table), but some people still wanted the best table, with the highest visibility, which was never by the window. Common people could see through the glass and that was not the audience these people played for. They played for each other.

"What about Irene?" Chloe asked, scanning the list. "She won the Tony last year, best lead in a musical."

"That was *last* year," Danny said. "She didn't win this year."

He crossed her name off the list and the work began. By the time they opened the doors for lunch a third of the names would be crossed out. Another third would have to go after discussing each one—the pros and cons, their relative importance in Margaret's orbit, and any damage they might do if they knew they'd been excluded. The first draft of the invitation list was highly confidential, a top secret document that had never fallen into the wrong hands and never would.

"Let's keep going," Danny said. He had to get invitations out by the end of the week for a party just a month away. He knew he should have started sooner, but he'd put it off. Saying goodbye to Margaret, then watching her go, was something he would prefer to put off forever, so he steeled himself, took a deep breath, and moved on to the next name.

9

The Arlington Hotel was a New York City landmark. First built in 1927, the hotel immediately became the preferred place to stay for anyone whose name was recognized by fans, voters, or readers of newspapers in wide circulation. It was also the place for those who aspired to be known, regardless of the slim odds. Hemingway had stayed here, as had the Governor of New York and, on several occasions, presidents of the United States.

New York City was unrecognizable now from what it had been in the Arlington's heyday. Times Square had become sanitized, and the New York Times, for which the Square was named, has moved several blocks over. The Gray Lady, as it had been called for a century, was not gray anymore and the building that housed the paper has been converted into high priced condominiums. Most of Manhattan, it seemed, has been transformed into a playground for the rich and famous. That was fine with D; he fancied himself among them, even though he wasn't that wealthy and planned to never be famous for what he was best at. He was content for his select clientele to know him as the proprietor of a men's clothing store that catered to the crème de la crème. They would never know he was much more well known—albeit in a completely anonymous way—as the Pride Killer. The police thought he was dead, or that he'd vanished or simply given up his one true passion. At least that's what they had thought until

Tuesday morning, when his first victim in three years was found floating past the United Nations.

D had never stayed at the Arlington. There was no reason for someone who lived in New York City to stay there, let alone someone who owned a townhouse within a long walk's distance from the hotel. It was true he'd met a few clients in the hotel's restaurant, mostly older men who thought a $2,000 suit was on the low end. He'd shied away from the nouveau riche, the rappers and the winners of television singing competitions. He wanted to keep his profile low; he was known for being discerning and discreet, and many of the newly wealthy were anything but.

He was sitting in the lobby of the Arlington enjoying a decaf cappuccino. He normally did not drink coffee, preferring a small variety of teas, but he would treat himself to something decaffeinated on special occasions, and this morning was one of them: he was waiting to meet one of two (count them, two!) prospective candidates for his next killing. And the candidate was late. D chalked it up to youth. Kevin (if that was his real name) was barely thirty and today was his day off. D checked his watch: ten minutes past eleven. Kevin was supposed to be there promptly on the hour. D realized, of course, that Kevin might not show up at all—it happened. But he would give the young man another ten minutes, then leave. He had his second interview that afternoon. He'd scheduled the killing for Thursday evening. It was possible that Kevin would not be free that night, which would factor into his decision. He was on a timetable. Fortunately, he had two very different men to choose from and there was a high probability one of them would be available. D was an expert at enticement. He would listen carefully as he chatted with each of the men, and if there was anything in what they said—a new movie out they wanted to see, or a favorite artist in a musical genre—he would be sure to let them know he was interested in that very thing. What a coincidence! He has a signed album of Patsy Cline's at home, or he'd gotten his hands on a pre-release DVD of the movie that was opening that very night. These were the perks of being a man who catered to men of the highest order. He would demure—it's nothing, really—and at the very least invite them over to his home that evening. They would ask for the address and he would insist on meeting for a drink first. He never gave his address to his victims. They might tell someone where they were going, or leave a note on the apartment desk they would never see again. Aside from his store manager Jarrod, the only people who knew where he lived did not survive to tell anyone.

D was getting impatient now. He glanced at his watch: 11:17 a.m. Three more minutes and he would have to leave. He was disappointed and was just about to write off Kevin as a fake or a no-show when a young man entered the lobby, harried and moving as if he was late for something, which he was.

"Leo?" he said, walking up to D.

D included his dead uncle's name among his aliases. He changed them up in the event someone overheard them talking. One day he was Leo, the next he might be Edward.

"That would be me," D said, standing and extending his hand. He'd told Kevin where he would be sitting but had not included a photograph of himself. He did not want any pictures floating around. Untraceable email accounts were one thing, photographs quite another. Instead he played shy with them, insisting he had no recent photos but guaranteeing them they would not be displeased, which they never were. He was in shape, average height, with graying brown hair he kept cut every week. He had bright blue eyes and a disarming smile (disarming them was of high importance). And when he smiled, whether for a client at the store or a candidate for his basement, he always made sure to include his eyes. A smile that does not extend to the eyes was a smile to be distrusted.

"I'm so sorry I'm late," Kevin said. "There was a sick passenger on the subway and we were in the station forever."

"Don't worry," D said. "These things happen. Please, have a seat."

Kevin sat down across from D. It was a small low table with two chairs, not for dining but for enjoying a beverage and conversation.

D looked at the man, quite pleased. Kevin was young, shorter than D would have liked, but with an open face and well-groomed. He struck D as neither noticeably masculine nor feminine, a balance he found in many men.

"Coffee?" D said. Kevin nodded and D waved at the waiter who served people in the lobby. There weren't many places like the Arlington left where gentlemen could sit and talk in a relaxing atmosphere.

"Staten Island is a long commute," said D. "It must take up a good part of your day going back and forth."

"I'm used to it," Kevin said. "I've never really wanted to live in Manhattan. It's too ..."

"Hectic."

"Yeah, hectic. I get enough of the city's energy just working at the bank. What was it you said you do?"

"Real estate. If you ever decide to move into the city, I'm your man."

Kevin gave his coffee order to the waiter, then took a moment for a good look at D.

"You're very nice looking," Kevin said.

"I try."

"This isn't something I normally do, meet men online."

"Nor I. But a friend has been encouraging me ever since my wife died."

"Oh, you had a wife."

"To whom I was faithful until she died three years ago. Then I decided it was time to be true to myself. I'd always known, you see, but never acted on it."

D liked to present himself as somewhat of a novice. He also knew that some men were turned on by sleeping with married men—or in this case widowed.

They talked for another twenty minutes. Kevin told D much about his life, how he'd grown up on Staten Island and taken his job at the bank three years ago. Working at a bank wasn't his dream but it was a job, and jobs these days were more important than ambitions. Besides, he'd worked his way up quickly from teller to branch manager, and it could be a career if he wanted it to be.

D told him all about his fictitious life as a Manhattan real estate broker, the pressures of selling multi-million dollar apartments, and the stresses of living in an Upper East Side penthouse.

"Those are some stresses I might like to have," Kevin said.

D watched as the young man's interest in him grew the more he told him about his wealth, position and prestige. Ah, youth, he thought, so easily lured.

Kevin was proving to be a prime candidate. D did not think of them as targets, but as interviewees for the most important position they would ever hold: provider of D's greatest pleasure in life. The pleasure itself only lasted for an evening, but gave D a lifetime of precious memories.

D was leaning heavily toward Kevin and was considering canceling his drink date with Scott that afternoon when Kevin's phone buzzed. He'd had the courtesy to turn the ringer off but he'd left it on vibrate.

"Sorry," Kevin said, taking his phone out of his shirt pocket.

"No problem," D replied, but it was a problem. He waited to see what Kevin said to whoever had called him. If he gave a location or any information that might lead to D, things would change quickly.

"Hi, Mom," Kevin said. He held up a finger to say, "Just a minute," to D and walked over to a corner to speak to his mother.

This was not a good turn of events. D had no way of knowing what Kevin was saying to his mother. Worse, *he was talking to his mother.* What grown man speaks to his mother while he's meeting another man for sex? It was the kind of call you would let go to voicemail, unless you mother's place in your life was overly prominent.

Kevin ended the call and came back, saying, "My apologies, really. My mom's alone now. My dad passed away five years ago from leukemia. I don't have any siblings, so I'm all she's got. I kind of have to take her calls."

Normally this sort of story would not effect D. Life was full of minor tragedies and heartache. But something about a young man as the only living family for a widow who was probably not much older than D himself troubled him. He never gave any thought to the survivors; sentimentality was not an asset in the serial killer business. But something just felt wrong this time.

"Where does your mother live?" D asked as Kevin sat back down.

"With me."

"With you?"

"Well, to be honest, I live with her. It's my parents' house."

D waited a moment. "You live at home?"

"Yeah, it saves a lot of money and it helps my mom. Is that a problem?"

"Not at all," D said, having decided it was. For all his youthful charm and attraction, Kevin was not the one for him. He hid his disappointment, as he hid all his emotions. (People mistakenly think sociopaths don't have emotions, but of course they do. Excitement, exhilaration, joy at the kill and sadness when it was over until the next time—were these not emotions?)

Kevin could sense things had taken a bad turn. "Listen," he said, "I really like you, Leo …"

"And I like you, Kevin, very much. I just have some other business to attend to today. How about if I send you an email this evening and we see where it goes?"

"Oh, okay, sure." Kevin had been blown off before, he knew what was happening.

D waved for the check. Kevin dug in his pocket for his wallet and D said, "This one's on me."

"Fine," said Kevin. "I'll get the next one."

He knew there would not be a next one. What he did not know was that his life had just been spared.

They parted ways with a handshake in front of the Arlington. D waited while poor, forlorn, rejected Kevin made his way up the block.

He did not want Kevin seeing which direction he took. He glanced at his watch. He was not scheduled to meet Scott until five-thirty.

It was going to be a long afternoon.

10

D did not know when he became a killer, only when he began to kill. It was as if the impulse had always been with him but never satisfied until he shoved his uncle down the stairs and the sight of him with his neck broken, his head twisted strangely perpendicular to his body, that he realized the full pleasure of what he had only fantasized until then. He had not tortured animals as a child; he had not set fires. He had been a fairly obedient boy, doing as he was told by his parents. Then his father left them and his mother sank into an acidic bitterness that corroded their lives. By the time D was fifteen he'd had enough—enough of his mother's toxicity, enough of her complaining about the world. He also knew very well she had little attachment to her son. He reminded her in too many ways of the man who'd walked out on her for another man. He had the same name, the same basic physical features, the same eyes.

"It's not my fault," she would say, for no apparent reason and out of context to anything they had been discussing. He knew it came from her deep belief of the opposite: that if she had been enough, if she had been a better wife, if she had done some crucial *something* differently her husband would have stayed and they would have had the ideal life he'd promised her in America. He knew, too, that she blamed him somehow, as if having a child had set them on the course to ruin—at least the ruin of her life.

D was startled when his mother announced she was going back to Berlin and gave him the options of going with her or moving to Brooklyn to live with his uncle. None of this had been discussed with him, and by the way she presented it he could tell which choice she preferred. D was part of the life she'd come to hate. D was unwelcome. D reminded her too much of the source of her anger.

"He has a nice apartment and a spare room. You could live in New York City, imagine how exciting that will be."

Not "would be," but "will be," as if the decision had been made for him.

D was relieved. He did not want to move to Germany, and the thought of being free from his mother's stifling emotions and her increasingly erratic behavior made him think escape was in sight. So on that rainy September morning he said goodbye to the woman he'd taken to calling Marta and boarded a plane for New York.

D's father began sending him letters a year after he moved to Brooklyn. He wanted to make amends, he said. He wanted to reconnect. He was living happily in San Francisco with Samuel and they had started a card shop together. A card shop! Rainbow Spirit was the name of the store. D hated it immediately. He also hated that the letters arrived in a variety of custom cards that Samuel made and sold at their store. It was quite a change from working in a Boeing factory.

His uncle Leo would hand him the cards using just his thumb and index finger, as if the cards might carry something nasty on their envelopes. Leo was on his sister Marta's side, even if he would never, ever, consider moving back to Germany. He was an American now, with citizenship and a thriving tailor business. D found out that Leo had offered to take them both in, but Marta had refused. She said America was a cruel and lonely place for cruel and lonely people. D came to believe her, at least about the cruelty.

D's father also had the temerity to include photos. There was his father and Samuel at the wharf. There was his father and Samuel in front of the card shop. There was his father, Samuel and a half dozen friends at a Pride parade. *A Pride parade?* What, D wondered, was there to be proud of in leaving your wife and young son in a wasteland? What was there to be proud of in opening a pitiful card shop with rainbows, triangles and pink shit all over the place? Pink shit. Pride shit. Rainbow shit. It was all shit to D, and the more he stared at the photos of his father and Samuel, the more he wanted to kill them both. *You did this to me,* he thought. *I'm living with an old man in Brooklyn, sewing suits for men who would wipe us from the bottoms of their shoes if they found a better tailor, a better clothier. I have no friends.* The only thing good to come out of it for D was that he loved New York City. He loved the vastness of it, its famed anonymity. He loved the tides of people swelling its streets. He loved the variety, the diversity, and, as time passed, its great opportunity. You could kill someone here and, depending on who it was, they would never be missed. You could set up shop with the most select customers imaginable and when the bodies were found no one would ever come around asking questions. That is, if you were cunning, careful and meticulous. If you were D himself.

He became aware of his sexuality in high school. He'd known much younger that other boys caught his eye, but at first he experienced it as a fascination rather than an attraction. He was fascinated by all things male. He liked the shape of men, the sound of men, the smell of men. By the time he was thirteen he was not interested in anyone his own age. He preferred to spend time at the barbershop, and he would purposely go when it was busiest, at lunch time or at the end of the work day. He would get in the back of the line and sit, pretending to read a newspaper, just so he could prolong his stay. He would sit and breathe the men in, the smell of the aftershave and many times their sweat.

He continued his visits to barber shops after he moved to Brooklyn. Some people liked libraries, some people liked restaurants. D liked the barber shop. By the time he was eighteen he was aware that some of the men looked at him with more than passing glances. He was a handsome teenager and looked a few years older than he was. Ripe, he thought. Ripe for the picking. But in his private thoughts (aren't all thoughts private?), he knew they were the ripe ones and he would someday do the picking.

He did not consider himself gay. Gay to D was an identity, and it was not his. He was instead same-sex attracted. That is how he had always defined it for himself. His father was gay. Samuel was gay. Parades and card shops and mannerisms and magazines were gay. D had no use for any of those things ... yet.

Then, when he was thirty-two years old, he killed his uncle. It wasn't very gratifying. His uncle was a good man. His uncle had been kind and offered D a place to live. His uncle had taught him the business and opened a store with both their names on it. But his uncle was in the way. He'd also begun asking D why there were no women in his life. *Because I'm not interested in killing women,* he'd wanted to say. Instead he offered the well-worn excuse that he hadn't met the right woman. He did not want to end up in a bad relationship or, worse, divorced like his parents. And besides, Uncle, we have too much work to do, too many things to accomplish together. Then the stairs and the broken neck, and he could finally set about making the life he wanted.

Becoming the Pride Killer was an accident of timing, really. He hadn't planned or anticipated making himself one of the most successful serial killers in New York City history at the same time all the gay people were celebrating. It had just been an auspicious day. He'd met the man named Oscar at a bar that catered to older gentlemen who liked younger ones. D was the younger one in the crowd that night, and within a few hours he had convinced the man to go home with him. His apartment was just a few blocks way. They could have another drink there in privacy. Sure, said Oscar, and fifteen minutes later they were in the townhouse D had purchased with his uncle's life insurance. It had given him enough for a down payment at a time before real estate reached the stratosphere. It was a fixer-upper, and D had fixed it up nicely, especially the basement.

He invited Oscar in and quickly offered him a cocktail. Oscar, having already consumed several drinks, gladly acquiesced. And then, finally, it was a trip to the basement to show Oscar his wine collection. Such a refined man to have a wine collection, and so young! Oscar was impressed and followed him down the stairs. He came back up in a large duffel bag.

The next day D realized, as he waited for news of the floater in the East River, that it was Pride weekend. Talk about perfect timing! He quickly formulated his plan and by the time of the festivities that always followed the parade he was known as the Pride Killer. Some clever reporter at the New York Herald had deemed him that. He thought it was appropriately tawdry, given his low opinion of all things Pride. He might have thought of a better name for himself but it stuck and he'd become fond of it. It was also when he decided on killing in threes.

He'd had to move quickly after Oscar. He found another victim on Thursday night, and a final on Saturday. No more from the bars. The internet made risks much easier to take, provided you had the sense to cover your tracks—and D had always been a man of uncommon sense.

That was seven years ago. He had not been caught, not even close. Some of his success he attributed to having been older when he started, in his mid-thirties. He was not youthfully impulsive. He planned carefully and executed (pun intended) his plan to the T. Or to the D, depending on how you look at it.

He was as professional at killing as he was at providing top-flight suits to top-flight men who had no idea the tailor measuring their inseams could kill them in sixty seconds. He had taken three years off to watch his mother disintegrate in a dreary Berlin apartment, two Pride weekends without their namesake's killer, and now he was back. His mother was dead. His father still sent him letters he left unanswered and immediately shredded—though both the card shop and Samuel were gone. He had a thriving men's store, a townhouse, and above all a career as the Pride Killer. He'd thought of retiring, especially since he had not been caught and wanted it to stay that way. But not yet. Maybe next year, or the year after that. For now he had two more victims to select and set free into oblivion. He saw himself as doing them a favor. Life was grief, anger and tears, for those weak enough to cry. D had never cried in his life.

11

The Stopwatch Diner was a Manhattan landmark specific to the area of Penn Station, where it had been in business since the mid-1940s. A gaudy neon stopwatch graced the front entrance, forever frozen at the ten-second mark above the front door. Inside it was much like a thousand other diners across America, but done in a racing motif: checkered flags on the walls, giant framed photos of famous race car drivers spewing champagne into the air.

Linda and Kyle had eaten here before, on her last trip to the city to see Kyle's photography exhibit. It was also where Danny had confronted his nemesis, Linus Hern, the restaurateur who'd hated him for years and who had conspired to secretly buy, through intermediaries, Margaret Bowman's building and the restaurant that bore her name. Danny had thwarted that scheme, found himself owning Margaret's Passion, and finally discovered why Linus was set on revenge: Danny had been hired by Margaret to replace Hern's young boyfriend ten years earlier. Sal was his name, and he took the loss of his position hard. He'd slipped back into addiction and finally gotten sober with a plunge off the 59th Street Bridge. Linus Hern blamed Danny, who'd had no part in it or knowledge of it, and set his sights on vengeance he almost achieved.

"Whatever happened to Linus Hern?" Linda asked as she and Kyle settled into a booth. The diner was full to capacity—it always was. A steady stream of customers came through the doors fresh off their trains, joining tourists who read about the Stopwatch on travel websites, and not a few locals who liked the moderate prices and the atmosphere.

"I don't know," said Kyle. "After the situation with Margaret's Passion he vanished. The last I heard he'd moved to Philadelphia."

"Maybe he got it out of his system, that whole business with Danny."

"I don't think Linus ever gets anything out of his system. I think he just moved on. I'd guess there were opportunities in Philly and he headed that way. He could smell an opportunity the way a predator smells blood."

A waiter came over to them to take their order. They'd been handed menus by the maître d' when she seated them. It was lunch time and both ordered club sandwiches, Linda getting tuna and Kyle the turkey. The waiter nodded and hurried off. Everything moved very quickly at the Stopwatch; meals were served and tables turned over in record time, and Kyle wondered if the staff were all being timed. It was the Stopwatch Diner, after all.

"Your boss is something else," Linda said. "It has to be a challenge working for her."

"It has been, and it's a challenge I'll miss."

"She's leaving?"

"Eventually. And I can't blame her. She was just about on the career skids when she covered the Pride Lodge murders. That made her a star of sorts. Then the bosses in Tokyo moved her into covering the city, and now she's a B-list reporter in a very niche market. She wants out of the niche before she's too old to make another move."

"What will you do if she leaves New York?"

"Stay," said Kyle, looking down at the checkered placemat. He did not want to talk about his boss's future, which would mean talking about his own. "How's Kirsten's mother?"

Dot McClellan had been hit by her third bout with cancer and this one she was rapidly losing. Linda was amazed that Dot had made it nine months, but neither she, Kirsten, nor Dot's oncologist expected Dot to see August.

"It's been very hard on Kirsten," Linda said. "Sometimes I think it was too much change for one person. She sold her interest in McClellan and Powers, she moved into the house with me, and her mother's dying."

McClellan and Powers Real Estate, the successful Bucks County business Kirsten had established with Madeleine Powers twenty years ago, was now just Powers Real Estate. The house they lived in was Linda's in Kingwood Township, five wooded acres just a mile away from the Delaware River but a world away from New Hope, where Kirsten had owned a condominium. Kirsten had not looked for another profession; she was consumed with her mother's care and her frequent trips to Phoenix, where Linda would be joining them Monday.

"The wedding was lovely," Kyle said, wanting to brighten things if he could. He and Danny had gone to New Jersey for the women's intimate ceremony and met Dot McClellan on the last trip she would ever take.

"Nothing like yours," Linda replied.

"Well ... we had more in-laws, and a lot more people locally who had to be invited. If it had been up to me and Danny we would have just gone to City Hall."

"But it was up to you."

"Tell that to our mothers."

The food arrived and they began eating, both of them welcoming a break in the conversation. The topics had been difficult ones, and Kyle was hoping to steer things back to Linda's visit to the city, the things she wanted to see this time and the places Kyle never went to unless they had company.

"We could take the ferry to the Statue of Liberty," Kyle said, picking just a handful of french fries from the plate and separating most of them into a pile he would not eat.

"I hear there's a sex museum," Linda said, smiling.

"Really? You want to see the sex museum?"

"It's a thought."

The waiter returned with a pot of coffee and Kyle placed his hand over his cup—he'd had three cups already today and was feeling jittery. The waiter dashed away to the next table.

"I was thinking ..." said Linda.

"Yes?" Kyle knew where this was going and wished they'd stayed on the topic of their weddings, or even Linda's mother-in-law.

"If this Pride Killer strikes every week this time of year ..."

"Yes."

"And the first victim was found in the river Tuesday morning ..."

"Yes."

"Then there's a second victim coming. Probably one he hasn't killed yet, or maybe not even identified."

Kyle sighed. It was a sigh of surrender. He knew as well as Linda did they had to do something. The police had never caught the Pride Killer and hadn't even had a suspect as far as Kyle knew.

"Where would we start?" he said, not looking up from his plate. His mind was working, trying to map out a strategy.

"He dumps the bodies in the river on the Upper East Side."

"Maybe he owns a car and drives them there from Long Island."

"Too risky."

"So maybe he has an accomplice, and the accomplice drives them there from Long Island."

"You're not keeping it simple," Linda said. "I think he feels invincible. He's gotten away with this for years, from what you told me. I think he stays close to home."

"Well the cops must think it, too, and look what they've come up with! Zero."

"We don't have much time."

Kyle thought another moment. "We have to talk to Vinnie."

"Your doorman? You said he was out on leave."

"I didn't say we had to talk to him at our building."

"You want to go where he lives. Is that information you have?"

"It's information I can get," Kyle said. "I'll just say I want to send a food basket. Joseph will give me his address." Joseph was the day-shift doorman and had been on the job for twenty-five years.

"So let's go," Linda said. "The stopwatch is running."

Kyle waved at the waiter and made the sign of a pencil in the air, the universal gesture of asking for a check.

Two minutes later they'd left the Stopwatch, walking quickly west on 32nd Street. Kyle thought of grabbing a taxi but decided they could use the time to think, plan, and work through the questions they would pose to a grieving, fragile Vincent Campagna. It was a delicate situation. Vinnie's brother had just been found bloated and floating in the East River. They would have to be gentle. At the same time, they needed answers quickly. Victor Campagna was the first of three as far as they knew. They hoped they were right, that Victor had not been the second while the first was still undiscovered somewhere.

12

The slowing of time is a phenomenon D was familiar with. Just as time can seem to pass ever more quickly, especially with age, it can also seem to drag, slower and slower, when one wants to be where one is not. Coming home from a trip, watching the clock as the workday passes, or waiting to meet someone who promises to fulfill your dreams. D dreamed of his next victim. He dreamed of the dance, the delicate charade as he pretended to be the man everyone thought he was while his true self slowly emerged. A conversation, a drink, a visit to the basement, and all would be revealed.

He had returned to his store after the long walk back from the Arlington. He'd been disappointed—not crushingly so, but enough that he wanted time to think and clear his head. It had happened before over the course of his career and his life. He'd had to wait for years while he grew into manhood, years more for the opportunity to be rid of his uncle. And the worst waiting of all, in a dreadful Berlin, waiting for his mother to surrender her bitterness and her regret and finally free him. He'd had to wait, too, for a replacement victim when his first choice didn't work out, twice that he could remember. But it always fell into place. It always came together, and it would this time, too.

"How did it go?" Jarrod asked. It was a slow afternoon. Keller and Whitman was never overly busy. It wasn't that kind of store and did not cater to that kind of customer. This was not the Gap.

"Pardon?" D asked. He was going through the racks of suits, making sure none were wrinkled, the price tags were pristine.

"With your client."

"Oh. You mean prospective client. Well, Jarrod, we win some and we lose some. He wasn't for us."

Jarrod knew not to question his boss further on the matter. Deidrich Keller did not like losing customers, even ones who never bought anything.

"I suggested he try Men's Warehouse." That said it all. The man had likely balked at the prices at Keller and Whitman. It was not a store for those who could not truly afford it. Sometimes they *thought* they could. They put on airs, they wasted Mr. K's time with meetings at hotels. They'd seen some celebrity wearing a suit from the store and imagined having a closet full of them. Then they realized it would set them back two months' rent or a trip to Disneyworld and they tried to bargain. Mr. K did not bargain.

"Easy come, easy go," Jarrod said.

"Indeed," D said.

He looked at his watch—there was no clock in the store. It was now 2:30 p.m. and he had another three hours before meeting Scott. He'd suggested drinks at a piano bar in the Theater District that was always filled with tourists—just the kind of witnesses he liked if there were any at all. Tourists did not stay around long and were scattered to the wind by the time the police came around asking questions. He'd never been to this bar and would not go again after interviewing Scott. He'd been careful all these years never to be seen in the same establishment twice. Fortunately, Manhattan had enough places to go that this was not a problem.

"I'll be leaving early this evening, Jarrod," he said. Normally he would stay until the store closed at 8:00 p.m. His uncle Leo used to stay open much later, always hoping to catch one more sale for the day, but D thought it made them look cheap. Souvenir shops stayed open till midnight, not fine men's clothing stores.

"Someone special?" Jarrod asked. He was careful to keep his few personal inquiries gender neutral. Mr. K had never spoken of his romantic life, if he had one, and Jarrod knew not to pry. But every now and then he would ask this sort of question. He liked his boss and hoped he would someday meet someone special, whether a man or a woman.

D looked at him and said, "The only special person in my life died in Berlin, Jarrod. I'm still grieving."

"But of course, my apologies for asking."

"No need to apologize, I know you mean well. But no, no one special. I just have plans, Jarrod. Even lonely, single men have plans."

Jarrod blushed. He regretted having asked about it. It was none of his business, none at all.

D glanced at his watch again. Ten minutes had passed since the last time he checked it. Time had slowed to a crawl. He decided to use some of it to practice what he would say to Scott, how he would get him to the townhouse, and what he would do if Scott, too, was not the right one. He doubted that would happen. He needed Scott to be the right one, and he was sure he was. He knew from experience that sometimes you had to settle. He wasn't expecting that, but if it happened, he would take what he could get.

13

The lunch crowd at Margaret's Passion was thinning. It was never especially busy, given the restaurant's location in Gramercy Park—there were no office buildings to supply a stream of executive assistants and the bosses whose every whim they catered to. There also weren't many tourists, except the ones on walking tours of the area.

Gramercy Park was a historic district that was once a swamp. A developer named Samuel B. Ruggles proposed the idea for a park in the early 1800s, when Manhattan was just beginning to push northward. The property was called "Gramercy Farm" and Ruggles spent the then-vast sum of $180,000 to drain the swamp and landscape it around a square, deeding 66 parcels of land to various owners. Today Gramercy Park is held in common as one of Manhattan's two privately owned parks and the park itself is gated, with keys given to the owners of each of the 39 surrounding structures. The Lexington Avenue subway had even been forced to re-route to Park Avenue so as not to go beneath the park and upset the privileged tenants.

Among the residents of Gramercy Park are The Players and the Gramercy Park Hotel. The Players was founded by Edwin Booth, brother of James Wilkes Booth, best known for assassinating Abraham Lincoln. To walk the streets of Gramercy Park is to travel back in time, to see New York City as it once was. Small groups of tourists listen breathlessly, snapping pictures, as tour guides tell them stories of who lived in which building and what moments in American history were acted out along its streets. It's not the sort of neighborhood where you'll find throngs of gawkers looking for neon signs, cheap souvenirs and Broadway celebrities.

It is where you'll find Margaret's Passion, there on a corner where Margaret Bowman first opened the restaurant in 1983. Like the neighborhood, little has changed about it—and Margaret always knew her customers liked it that way. A Who's Who of New York City society has dined there for three decades—mayors, fashion designers, even the President of the United States on several occasions. But just as importantly, it has served the local residents of Gramercy Park all that time. They like its familiarity and its comfort. They like its elegant, old-looking interior. And they love Margaret Bowman. Danny could not imagine Margaret's Passion without Margaret, and even though she seldom made the trip downstairs from her apartment to visit table to table as she'd done for years, they knew she was around, watching over them. Danny knew once she was gone they would rely on the restaurant staying the same. It was a bone of contention he had with Kyle's mother Sally. She didn't want to completely change the place, but she thought it needed "refreshing," as she put it. He disagreed and was planning to have a long talk with her—soon.

The restaurant closed at 2:00 p.m. and reopened for dinner at 6:00 p.m.. Chloe was getting things ready for the daily transition, changing out the menus and making sure the setup was done meticulously, with the help of Trebor the bartender. Danny had hired them both, and they had repaid his decision with loyalty and professionalism. He was sitting at the bar, having a cup of coffee, watching them. He remembered being new to the restaurant himself, hired by Margaret. Poached, really, from another restaurant, but she'd seen something in him she liked and wanted at Margaret's Passion. She had not been wrong.

"She knows you're coming," Chloe said.

"Of course she does," Danny replied. He made the trip upstairs to visit with her almost every day now. Her decision to move to Florida had been made, but Danny and Margaret had not yet talked about it in more than the abstract. The way people talk around things they would rather not discuss in specifics. Specifics are very real. Specifics say, this is happening, there's no turning back.

Danny finished his coffee and headed into the kitchen where the staircase was leading up to Margaret's apartment. He nodded at Chef Cecily, who'd been brought on to replace Chef Jeff several months ago. Another excellent but hard decision (Jeff had been with the restaurant longer than Danny, but his father was ailing in Denver and he'd left to take care of him). He nodded at the dishwasher and the busboy, whose wives' names he knew and whose children's birthdays he remembered every year with gifts. It had been Margaret's way, and now it was Danny's. He climbed the back stairs, slowly, his eyes on the door at the top, wishing he would never get there.

"Hello, Danny," Margaret said, opening the door before he reached the top step. She always did, and he'd wondered many times how she knew he was coming just then. The stairs didn't creak, he didn't pound his feet. His ascent was silent, yet Margaret always knew he was coming and she always opened the door before he knocked.

"Good afternoon," Danny said.

The stairs led into Margaret's kitchen and she waved Danny in, closing the door behind him. There were two cups on the small kitchen table he'd sat at a thousand times, one with coffee for Danny, one with tea for Margaret. They were silent as Danny took his seat at the table. Silence was not something they shared often, but they both knew what was coming ... and who was going.

"I was thinking this morning," Margaret said, "how many times you've greeted me with 'Good afternoon' over the last eleven years."

"It used to be downstairs," Danny said.

Until the last two or three years Margaret had gone down to the restaurant every day, often during the lunch service to say hello to her customers, and always to greet the staff.

"A lot of things used to be, Danny."

She was right and he knew it, and it only made his heart heavier.

"That's what life is." She sipped her tea and smiled at him. "One day you wake up—in my case at eighty-two—and you realize pretty much everything you've experienced in your life 'used to be.'"

Margaret had adopted Danny, not legally but emotionally. She and Gerard never had children, and when she hired Danny she soon discovered he was exactly the kind of man she would like to claim as her son.

Danny took a sip of his coffee and cleared his throat. "I've been working on the list," he said.

"The list?"

"The list for your party a month from now."

Could it really be coming that soon, he wondered. Her life in New York, her years with the restaurant, her decade with him coming up those stairs to talk about menus and waiters and guest lists.

"Be sure to invite your parents," she said. "And Kyle's mother, if she'd like to come. And anyone else you'd like to have there."

He looked at her. "Seating's limited. If I invite the politicians and the celebrities and ..."

She cut him off with a shake of her head. "No, no, no, Danny. This one's for you more than it is for me. I don't care if any of those people are there. Unless you want them to come."

He stared at her. *This one's for you, Danny.* He knew then she understood just how hard this was for him and that she had asked for this going away party to give him the sense of an ending. It wasn't for Margaret. She could easily pack her bags and walk out the door tomorrow, but she wanted Danny to have this chance to say goodbye, and say it in a big way.

"Listen," she said, sliding her hand across the table and placing it over his. "I have something for you. Stay here a moment."

She got up from the table and shuffled into the living room, leaving Danny to look around the kitchen he'd seen so many times. Was there anything he'd missed? Had he ever heard the cuckoo strike time on the wall clock? He couldn't remember. Did he know what her view was through the small window above her sink? Had he ever stood there and looked to see?

Margaret came back in with a manila envelope. She sat down and handed it to him.

"What's this?" he said, afraid to open it. Was it her will? Was it a photograph of some moment in their lives together?

"Open it and see."

Danny pulled the flap back on the envelope and slid out a single piece of paper. It was a deed. He read it quickly, then said, "I don't understand."

"I have the money you gave me to buy the restaurant," she said. "It's more than I'll need to live another few years."

"Don't say that."

"Okay, Danny, maybe ten. Is that long enough?"

"Never is not long enough." He felt his eyes sting.

"I won't tell you not to cry. I don't know why people do that, it's wrong. We all need to cry."

He wiped his eyes with the back of his hand and looked at the paper again. She was giving him the building.

"I don't want the building," he said. "You have tenants. I'm not a landlord."

"And neither were we. Gerard had no idea how to be a landlord. So we hired a management company. You can do the same. Or you can sell it and do something else with the proceeds."

"I would never sell Margaret's Passion."

"But you might have to, if someone else owned the building. You see? This way that can't happen."

"I should talk to Kyle."

"So talk to Kyle. But the deed is done." She laughed at the pun. "And just think, my dear Danny, you'll be able to afford to buy out Sally Callahan soon."

Margaret knew Danny did not like being in business with his mother-in-law. If he owned the building, with the rent and even a line of credit against the equity, he could pay Sally back and have her return to being just Kyle's mother.

"I still don't understand."

"There's nothing to understand. I can't take the building with me, you know! And I don't need some albatross hung around my neck a thousand miles away."

"Is that how far Florida is?"

"Something like that."

"I've never been there."

"Well, now you'll have a reason to come."

And he would. Margaret was leaving in high summer and already Danny had imagined spending Christmas in Boca Raton. He and Kyle would be learning more about Florida with Margaret moving there than he'd ever wanted to know.

"Now let's go over this guest list," Margaret said.

"I didn't bring it with me."

"That's okay. We'll start a new one, and no one we once felt obligated to invite will be on it. This one's for us."

Margaret went to the kitchen counter, opened a drawer and took out a small writing pad and a pen she kept there for making grocery lists. She came back to the table and sat down.

"Danny, Kyle," she said, scribbling their names. "What about that sweet detective friend of yours? Would you like her there?"

"Yes," Danny said. "Linda Sikorsky. And she has a wife now, Kirsten."

"Oh does she? How lovely."

They began going over names then, Danny listing people he truly wanted at Margaret's going away party, and Margaret adding her own as she wrote the names down.

The weight of it began to lift slightly for him. He wanted the afternoon to stretch out endlessly, to spend every second he could sitting at Margaret Bowman's kitchen table, watching her elderly hand write names in a shaky scrawl. He glanced at the envelope. *Oh, Margaret, what have you gotten me into?* Everything stays the same, he thought, until it all changes.

14

When most people think of the New York City subway they imagine a vast underground labyrinth. Kyle had been no exception, and for his first year living in the city, some thirty years ago, he'd taken buses rather than descend beneath the earth to barrel through tunnels dug a century before. It had reminded him of Poe's "The Premature Burial." There was something about being alive down there that had frightened him, until he realized it was a much faster and more efficient way to travel, especially from his then-home in Brooklyn to the various jobs he held in Manhattan.

Not all the trains that snake around the boroughs are subterranean. The N train, on which Kyle and Linda rode to Astoria, glides under the river past its last stop in Manhattan and emerges in Queens to continue along elevated tracks. Once upon a time you could look out from the train windows and see the World Trade Center before it came tumbling down in a morning of terror. Kyle remembered the days immediately following, when a plume of smoke rose from the hole in the ground that had been the Twin Towers. He couldn't believe nearly thirteen years had passed since then.

Kyle and Danny went to Astoria almost every weekend to visit Danny's parents in their row house on 28th Street. He knew the neighborhood well. He knew the Kaufman Astoria Studios. He knew the Museum of the Moving Image, housed in the same complex. He knew Steinway Street, named after the world famous piano makers. And he knew the Greek feeling of the area, still populated by Greek families who had lived here for generations and who still gave Astoria its flavor. They were mixed now with Iranians, Pakistanis, pockets of other Middle Eastern immigrants, and not a few gay people. Astoria was once known for being both affordable and quite nice, and as Manhattan became ever more expensive and out of reach for the average person, Astoria became a favorite refuge. You could get a large one-bedroom, maybe even a two-bedroom, for what you would pay for a studio in Chelsea. The migration brought higher prices, and Astoria was no longer the hidden gem it once was, but still a very nice place to live just a stone's throw from Manhattan.

"I love the skyline," Linda said, looking out the window as the train eased along the tracks, turning and running parallel to the East Side.

"Everybody does," Kyle replied. And it was true. No matter how often he'd thought of leaving New York City, he never stopped being thrilled by the sight of it from a distance. "It may not be the greatest city in the world—don't tell New York that—but it's the greatest skyline. It calls to you."

Four stops in they pulled into the Broadway station. Broadway is a main artery in Astoria, running east to west. It's where you'll find grocery stores, shops, restaurants, real Greek diners, and all the other small businesses that make up a neighborhood. It's also three blocks from Vincent Campagna's apartment. Kyle had called and gotten the address from Joseph the doorman. He'd bent the truth and said he wanted to send a food basket to Vinnie (which he would, just not now). Joseph had no reason to suspect anything and had given Kyle the information. He said quite of few of the tenants had been asking. Word spread quickly about the tragedy of Vinnie's brother.

They walked east a block, turned and walked another two blocks south, and found themselves in front of a large brown apartment building with six stories. Astoria was full of them. Row houses and apartment buildings made up most of the dwellings here. And Kyle knew from friends who lived here that the apartments tended to be large. The buildings were what's called "pre-war" and came at a premium price across the river in Manhattan. It meant they were built before World War II, between 1900 and 1940, when space was plentiful and architecture still had a flare. They were also known for being very sturdy, just in case a hurricane decided to stop by.

"He's in 4C," Kyle said. They were standing in front of a buzzer box with dozens of apartment numbers on it, each with a name and button beside it. He buzzed Vincent's apartment.

"What if he's not home?" Linda asked.

"Joseph told me he was. Apparently he's the only one from the building Vinnie's been talking to."

Kyle waited a moment, pressed again, and they heard the front door buzzer go off, giving then entrance. Kyle quickly pulled the door open and held it for Linda.

The entryway was massive, as they often are in these buildings. It appeared large enough to hold fifty people, but it was completely empty except for the mailboxes along one wall. A wide staircase led up to the floors above them, and an old elevator stood along the back, next to an apartment Kyle guessed was the super's. Almost every apartment building in New York City has a super—the man (for it is inevitably a man), often with his family, who lives in and takes care of the building.

They took the elevator up to the fourth floor. Vinnie had not called down through the intercom to ask who was there and Kyle assumed the building didn't have one, or didn't have one that worked.

They stepped off the elevator and out onto a hallway. Apartment doors lined the walls in both directions. Taking a quick look at the first two, Kyle determined that Vincent Campagna lived three doors down to the right. They walked to the door and knocked.

Kyle was startled at first by Vinnie's appearance. He looked like a man who had not slept for two days, which was the case. He was on the short side, about five-five, with dark, almost black hair that had not been washed recently. He also hadn't shaved, and a thick stubble covered the lower half of his face. He was wearing a t-shirt that said Key West on it, jeans and no shoes or socks.

"Mr. Callahan," he said, surprised to see Kyle.

"Vinnie, please call me Kyle."

Vinnie looked at Linda.

"This is my friend, Detective Linda Sikorsky."

Linda was surprised Kyle introduced her that way and guessed he was doing it for a reason.

"I spoke to the police already," Vinnie said. "A couple times."

"She's not with the New York City police. She's visiting Danny and me from New Jersey. May we come in?"

"Oh, sure, sure." Vinnie stepped aside and waved them in. "Don't mind the mess."

What mess, Kyle wondered, as they entered the apartment. Vinnie Campagna was neat and orderly, among his other traits. The apartment was a studio, with a murphy bed folded up into one wall, a small dining table beneath a window, and a comfortable couch and chair in one corner. A television was on but muted, with a news channel playing.

"I'd offer you something …"

"No, Vinnie, that's fine," said Kyle. "We won't stay long. Linda just wanted to ask you some questions."

I did? Linda thought. She wished Kyle had told her before they got there.

"Yes, well," Linda said, improvising as she sat in the chair with Kyle and Vinnie taking the couch. "I was wondering …"

Kyle saw the hesitation. "She was wondering what you could tell us."

"What I could tell you?"

"About the last time you spoke to Victor."

Vinnie thought about it. He didn't know what difference it would make, since he'd been over these details with the police, but anything that might help find his brother's killer was worth it.

"It was Monday," he said. "I was at home in the afternoon. Vic's on a dayshift at 230 Park" – that was the apartment building Victor worked at – "and he was off Mondays and Tuesdays. He was excited about our niece's christening on Saturday. Ah, Christ, that's been postponed."

"I'm sorry," Kyle said. "But please go on. You spoke Monday?"

"Yeah, for a few minutes. We talked every day. We were very close." He stopped a moment, composing himself. "Vic wanted a new suit for the christening and said he was going to look for something nice."

Linda had taken her phone out and was making notes on one of its applications.

"But he was stopping for a drink first," Vinnie continued. "Said he was meeting a friend at Cargill's."

"What's Cargill's?" Linda asked.

"It's a bar. A gay bar. On East 58th Street."

Kyle knew of the place. It was one of the oldest gay bars on the East Side, and one of the few remaining. Kyle remembered it as a local watering hole that catered to a neighborhood crowd. No go-go dancers, no drag shows. Just booze and companionship.

"Do you know the name of the friend he was meeting?"

"No, sorry. Vic was out of the closet, but very … discreet, I guess you'd say. He had boyfriends from time to time but never brought them around. He wasn't uncomfortable being gay, he just didn't feel like he belonged anywhere. The gay scene, whatever that is, it wasn't for him and he was still looking for his place in the world. Now he'll never find it. But he liked that bar, yeah, something about it."

"Did you hear from him after that?" Linda asked.

"No."

"And what time was your conversation?"

"About three o'clock, sometime in there."

Kyle hesitated. He didn't want to bring up anything that would make Vinnie uncomfortable.

"Do you know if Vic ever met men online?"

Vinnie stared at him. "For hookups, you mean?"

"Or dates. Dinner, a movie, whatever. People meet online all the time."

"Is that how you met Mr. Durban?"

"Danny," Kyle said. "You can call him Danny. You're not on duty, Vinnie. And no, I didn't meet Danny online. We met at an art gallery."

Vinnie nodded. "I don't really know if he met guys online," he said. "Vic was …"

"Discreet," said Linda.

"Yeah, discreet. I'm sure he did meet men that way. But it's not the kind of thing he would tell me."

"So your phone call on Monday was the last."

Vinnie didn't answer and looked about to cry. He glanced away a moment, not wanting to break down in front of these people.

"Yeah," he said at last. "I called him later to make plans for Saturday, we were going together to the christening. But it went to voicemail. Tried texting too but that didn't get a response. He was known to turn his phone off, especially on his days off. He liked to 'unplug' he said, walk around and just look at things, listen to sounds and other people's conversations. He had his head in the clouds sometimes, that kid. He was my little brother, did I say that? Three years younger."

"You didn't mention it, no," Linda said. "We're so sorry, Vinnie."

"Thanks." He took a deep breath. "So I talked to him Monday when he was going to Cargill's, and never again. Never will, either. You think they'll catch the guy who did this?"

Kyle did not answer immediately. He knew the Pride Killer had not been caught for four years before vanishing. "We're going to try," he said. Then, very gently, he asked, "Do you have a photograph of Vic?"

"A picture?"

"Yes," Linda said. "So we can ask around, see if anyone remembers seeing him on Monday."

"Sure, sure." Vinnie got up and crossed to a small bookshelf. He had several framed photographs of his family and friends. He took one of his brother, quickly slipped it out of the frame, and brought it back, handing it to Kyle. "It's a couple years old but this is what he looks like."

Kyle took the photograph, glanced at it and slipped it into his shirt pocket. "Thank you, Vinnie, thank you very much. I'll be sure to get this back to you. We're going to go now, but I really am terribly sorry for your loss."

"My loss? Vic's the one who lost. Lost it all. I just want to find the man who took it."

"We're going to do our best," said Linda.

Kyle and Linda rose and thanked Vinnie again for talking with them. Vinnie followed them to the door.

"He's not the only one, is he?" Vinnie asked as he opened the door for them.

Kyle had not wanted to tell Vinnie what he knew of the killer, his elusiveness and success. But Vinnie had spoken to them at the most difficult time of his life and was owed the truth.

"No, Vinnie, I'm afraid not," Kyle said. "But we're trying to make sure there won't be any more."

"Good luck," Vinnie said as they left the apartment. "You'll let me know, right? If you find him?"

Linda turned back and said, "You'll be the first to know. Then we'll call the morgue."

Kyle was struck by the coldness in her voice, and by the implication in her words. She was prepared to make sure the Pride Killer never claimed another victim. Dead predators can't hunt.

They left Vincent Campagna's building and headed back to the subway. As they climbed the stairs at the station, Linda said, "Where to now?"

"I could use a drink," Kyle said. "And I know just the place."

The train pulled into the station just as they reached the turnstiles. Kyle used his MetroCard to swipe them through, and together they rushed up the stairs. Even the ten minutes it would take for the next train to arrive was time they did not have to waste.

15

Ed Cargill opened Cargill's bar when he was just twenty-five and new to New York City. Back then the Upper East Side was an inexpensive part of the city to live in, which could be said of much of Manhattan in the late 1950s. Ed made his way from Dayton, Ohio, as a young gay man looking for a place to belong. He found it in New York. He also found it in the bar that bore his name, and even though he endured police raids and the pervasive discrimination of a society and its police force that thought homosexuality was a mixture of crime and illness, he loved his patrons and he loved his city.

Cargill's had weathered the storms and the decades, and though Ed had long since passed on to the Great Gay Bar in Heaven, the establishment he founded still served the locals who had come to know it as their bar. They weren't all gay, either. Cargill's was inclusive before inclusivity was in vogue. You can find gay customers there having an after-work cocktail with their straight co-workers, their bisexual co-workers and, increasingly, their transgender co-workers.

The interior remained understated and comfortable. This was no splashy Chelsea bar. There was no loud music. Ed had installed a jukebox that people still loved putting quarters in, playing records by Janis Joplin and Patsy Cline mixed with current music from the bartenders' mix-tapes. Cargill's managed to be a comforting friend without being a throwback. It was run now by Ed's nephew, himself a man in his 60s who'd made his way to New York when he was just out of college and needed a little coming out of his own. Phil Carter didn't work at the bar much and wasn't there when Kyle and Linda arrived, but he'd kept the place in almost exactly the same shape, look and feel his uncle had left it when he took over in 1995.

"So this is a gay bar," Linda said as they walked through the door.

Kyle was surprised. He knew gay life was new to Detective Linda, but he hadn't imagined she had not visited at least one bar since her coming out a year and a half ago. Then he remembered so much had changed with the advent of the internet. Gay bars were becoming an anachronism, and bars like Cargill's almost museum pieces.

"Yes and no," Kyle said. "There are lots of different kinds of gay bars. Not that I know. Danny and I don't go to bars and I was never much of a bar person before I met him. This is more like an old neighborhood bar with a more interesting clientele than most."

There were only a half dozen people there; it was the middle of the afternoon, and the few customers at the bar (with two at a pool table) were the types who either stopped by for a friendly drink or who never left.

A tall man in his 40s was behind the bar washing glasses and nodding to patrons who talked to him whether he listened or not. He was dressed in khakis and a green long-sleeved shirt with the cuffs rolled up to reveal several tattoos on his forearms.

"Afternoon," Kyle said as he and Linda each took a stool.

"Afternoon," said the bartender. He put down a glass and walked over. "What can I get you folks?"

"Diet Coke for me," Linda said and Kyle ordered the same.

When the bartender set their drinks on napkins, Kyle said, "We're looking for some information."

The bartender eyed them, but not suspiciously. He'd had plenty of people—police and others—who came in every now and then looking for information. Most were just tourists wondering how to get to the South Street Seaport or the Empire State Building. Occasionally he'd get a private investigator trying to track down someone's errant spouse.

"I'm Kyle, by the way. And this is Detective Linda Sikorsky."

The bartender came to attention. "Robert," he said. "Robert Jeffries."

"Yes, well, Bob …"

"Nobody calls me Bob."

"Sorry," said Kyle. "Robert … we were wondering if you saw this man on Monday afternoon."

Kyle pulled out the photograph of Vic Campagna and handed it to Robert. He took the picture and held it up to the light.

"Vic," he said. "Yeah, I knew Vic. Very fucked up, what happened to him."

"Very," Linda said. "We think he may have met someone here."

The implication was not lost on Robert. He glanced around, as if someone dangerous might be sitting at one of his bar stools.

He handed the picture back. "He was in here to meet his buddy Sam, but Sam's no killer. He never even showed up. I remember Vic waiting about a half hour. Then he said Sam stood him up again and he left."

"Sam stood him up?" asked Kyle. "Were they dating?"

"Dating? Ah, no. Sam's got a husband. They're just friends, as far as I know. They met here a couple years ago, I remember that. And once or twice a month they'd meet for drinks, get caught up I guess. I try not to eavesdrop."

"Does Sam have a last name?" Linda asked.

"Paddington. Fortyish, works at the Met I think. The museum, not the opera."

"Any idea where we might find Sam?"

"The museum," Robert replied dryly.

"Right," said Kyle. "Not the opera. Do you know what he does there?"

"He's a ticket-taker, maybe an usher, I'm not sure." Robert leaned closer. "Listen, you think this is that guy, that Pride Killer? I heard he died or something. I remember when he was doing this before. Very scary."

"No one knows what happened to him," Kyle said. "Only that he's back. *If* he's back. It could be a different killer. It could be random."

"Word's starting to spread. My customers are getting nervous. Some of them, they knew Vic, they knew he came in here."

"I have a feeling that's not how Vic met his killer. The internet's a much more likely place to meet men who don't want to be found."

"Or seen," Linda added.

"Right, right. Should I put up posters or something? You know, warn people?"

"That's up to you," said Kyle. "But it might start a panic. As long as people know to use their instincts and common sense."

"I never meet guys on the internet, and I don't hookup. It's crazy. I'm like, control your impulses already, you could get killed doing this. And now they got apps on phones, you can find some guy in the coffee shop sitting next to you."

Kyle had read about these things but knew nothing of them and didn't want to know. The only man he ever wanted to find was Danny, and that was easy enough.

"Listen, Robert, you've been very helpful," Kyle said. He slid off his barstool and Linda followed.

"You gonna talk to Sam?"

"It's a possibility."

"It's not him, I'm telling you. Sam's been coming in here for years. Quiet guy, not your hookup type either. And definitely not a killer."

"Thanks," said Linda. She threw a ten dollar bill on the bar. "Keep the change."

They left Robert standing there wondering if he'd served a drink to a murderer in the last three days and if he should sound some kind of alarm. Heading back out to 58th Street, Kyle stopped on the sidewalk and mulled over the information they had, which was next to none.

"So," Linda said.

"So ... Vic comes here to meet Sam, Sam doesn't show up."

"Do they text? Do they call?"

"The police will know, if they have Vic's phone. That's not the kind of information they put in news reports."

"Should we leave it up to them, then? The police?"

Kyle looked at her. "There's no time," he said. "For all we know Vic wasn't the first victim."

"Sam was. He didn't show up. It's possible there's some connection between the three of them—Vic, Sam and the Killer."

"Possible, yes. We have to look at everything as possible, although I have my doubts. It doesn't fit this killer's pattern, but neither does disappearing for three years."

"So you want to go to the Met?"

"Yes," said Kyle. "The museum, not the opera."

"But we don't know what Sam Paddington does there."

"Someone will tell us."

Kyle stepped to the curb and held up his hand. A taxi heading west pulled up within seconds, and they drove off after Kyle told the driver they were going to the Metropolitan Museum of Art.

16

D was uncharacteristically anxious. It was another thing that had changed since he was last in the hunt. First there had been the curious disappointment with killing Victor, as if he'd lost interest in the one thing he'd been most passionate about in his life. And now this anxiety, this impatience. He refused to believe he was *nervous*—that was for novices and people unsure of themselves. D was supremely confident in everything he did. This was more like a general anxiety, and it had gotten the best of him as he'd waited in the store, checking his watch every fifteen minutes. Finally, at 3:15 p.m., he'd told Jarrod he was feeling just a little under the weather and he wanted to go home and lay down for a bit.

"Is it something you ate?" Jarrod asked, concerned for his boss. He'd noticed a change in Mr. K since his return from Germany. He attributed it to the loss of his mother. Jarrod's mother had passed away six years ago, and he knew how difficult it could be. He'd learned that grief was not linear, that it came and went in waves. He suspected a wave had overtaken Mr. K and he just needed to be alone.

"No, I'm sure that's not the cause," D replied. "But thank you so much for asking, Jarrod. You're a true friend. I just want to rest awhile. I'll be fine in the morning."

D had left the store then, walking the three blocks to his townhouse. He wanted to center himself before meeting Scott. He was worried Scott, too, would not be the one, and he would find himself in a rush to identify a replacement. Rushing was dangerous. People who hurried made mistakes, and he could not be one of them. He walked briskly north toward home, wanting to get there quickly. He knew he would feel better once he was there—and not in his bed, as he had told Jarrod, but in his basement.

When D first bought the townhouse the basement had been dank and empty. It seemed people in New York had no imagination, no ability to see an empty cellar as anything but a place to put boxes or washing machines. D had taken a look and seen potential. It was one of the reasons he bought the place. He knew when he first descended the stairs that he could turn this space into something special. First to go were the rickety stairs. They were narrow and wooden and *looked* dangerous. The last thing he wanted anyone to think when they headed down the stairs was that something dangerous was waiting for them. No ghosts, no cobwebs, no rodents. New York City was full of rodents, D thought. Most of them with office jobs and cell phones to their ears.

He'd replaced the stairs with wider planks and had them carpeted. Carpet was essential in his redesign: it absorbed sound. It was also comfortable to walk on, and he wanted his victims to feel very comfortable when he took them downstairs.

Essentially the basement was whatever D needed it to be when he was chatting up his victims in the living room. He was adept at determining their pastimes and passions. One man was a wine connoisseur and, lo and behold, so was D! In fact, D had an impressive collection of wines in his basement, in a temperature controlled room. Come, I'll show you. Another collected jazz records from the 1950s. Really? You'll never believe this, but I have a collection as well in my basement. Come, I'll show you.

Whatever it was they fancied—photography, art, sculpture, movies—D had just the thing to impress them, down a short flight of carpeted stairs, down beneath his townhouse, down where no one but D ever came back from alive.

He'd furnished the basement, of course. Large leather chairs and a sofa. A wide-screen TV. Even a computer on a large desk. All for appearances. It was an illusion he only needed to sustain for a short while. By the time they got down there they were already woozy from a special cocktail in the living room. Something to refresh them and dull their senses. He'd only had to struggle with two of them, but he was in shape and it had never been a real contest.

D got home and went directly to his basement. It really was a very comfortable space, and he sometimes spent an afternoon or evening here by himself. He might watch the news, or listen to some music. He might have a drink, but never before a meeting. Today he simply wanted to center himself, to sit awhile in his favorite environment and let his mind slow down. He didn't like his thoughts racing. They could get away from him, which is what had happened earlier. He'd grown so impatient in the store that he'd become agitated, and his basement was the perfect place to remedy that.

He slipped off his shoes and sat back on the brown leather sofa. He imagined Scott being the one, coming over the next evening for a quick visit before heading off to dinner. He imagined Scott liking old movie posters and discovering to his delight that D had several originals ... in the basement. Greta Garbo, Humphrey Bogart. Signed by the illustrator, no less. Come, take a look.

He closed his eyes and luxuriated in mental images. Scott having a second drink ... *here, let me freshen that.* Scott needing to sit a minute, feeling lightheaded. Scott wondering what was happening to him just as D came up behind the sofa, his special belt taught between his hands, slipping the thick black leather over Scott's head as Scott realized there had indeed been something very dangerous down those stairs, something deadly.

D smiled, opened his eyes slightly, and looked at his watch. One more hour.

17

The Metropolitan Museum of Art is the largest art museum in the United States and one of the ten largest in the world. You can see its classical Greek columns as you approach its massive façade on Fifth Avenue, the steps leading up to the entrance crowded in good weather with tourists, students and sightseers from around the world. Banners heralding its exhibits drape down the front like giant flags. Founded in 1870 by a group of American businessmen, financiers, artists and leading thinkers of the day, the Met has been a must-see destination for people visiting New York City since its doors first opened.

The taxi pulled up in front of the museum, taking its place behind a long line of cabs dropping off and picking up passengers. Kyle paid the driver, noticing how much more expensive it had become to take a taxi. Just getting into the backseat will cost you $2.50, and if you go more than a few blocks you'll burn through $10 in the course of a very short conversation—your own, or the one the cab driver enjoys illegally on a cell phone plugged into his earpiece.

"Who was he talking to?" Linda asked as they headed up the museum steps.

"No idea," Kyle said. "I don't understand the language. And he's not supposed to be talking to anyone, it's against the law. Danny tells them to stop, but they all do it anyway."

Linda slowed down and looked up at the museum. She'd never been here and was as impressed as she was meant to be by the architecture. The museum had a Very Important Place feel to it and she was amazed by the sheer number of people on the steps, climbing up and down them, sitting on them, taking pictures and flowing into and out of the building.

"This looks like a museum you could spend a day in," Linda said as they entered.

"At least a day."

The main room was cavernous and even more crowded than the outside. Visitors herded in three directions, wandering with maps to the left, right, and up a wide set of stairs directly across from the front doors.

Kyle stopped once they'd cleared the entrance enough not to obstruct it. He'd had no plan and had not formed one on the way over.

"What are we going to do?" Linda asked.

"I'm thinking." Kyle looked around, wondering who to ask about a man named Sam Paddington. He worked here, but where? Doing what? The bartender at Cargill's said he might be a ticket taker. "Let's just get our tickets and figure this out."

They headed to one of several counters. This one was staffed by two young women who looked like they could be interns or volunteers, and an older man who appeared to be teaching them the ropes.

"Two adults," Kyle said, handing his credit card to the man. He knew the entrance fee was suggested (something most of the tourists didn't realize) but decided he would make the full donation and support his local art institution.

The man took Kyle's card and swiped it. Kyle pegged him as gay. It doesn't take that much to get the sensors reacting: a mannerism, a speech pattern. In this case, the man just seemed a little fussy. Kyle thought he was probably very good at his job—fussy is likely an attribute working at one of the most famous museums in the world.

"Excuse me," Kyle said, signing the credit card receipt.

"Yes?" said the man. "Did you need a map?"

"No, no. Actually, I'm looking for someone."

The man glanced around. "Good luck here, there are several thousand people to sift through. What does this person look like? I could keep an eye out for you, let them know you've arrived."

"Actually, I don't know what he looks like."

The man looked at Kyle, then at Linda, sizing them up. Probably one of those gay man/straight woman friendships, although Linda seemed like she could be family.

"I just have a name," Kyle said. "Sam Paddington. I'm told he works here at the museum."

The man's eyes widened. He cocked his head, most curious, then said, "I'm Sam Paddington."

"Seriously?" Linda said.

"Well, yes. Seriously, not seriously. Frivolously, depending on my mood. Why are you looking for me?"

Kyle took a moment to compose himself. People choose not to believe in coincidence, preferring the illusion of order only rarely disturbed by the unexpected, but coincidences happen all the time. Life, Kyle believed, was pretty much one long coincidence that appeared not to be.

"It's about Victor Campagna," he said.

Sam's expression froze. He looked quickly to the two young women at the counter with him. "Excuse me, Gina," he said to the girl on his left. "I'm going to step away for a few minutes."

"Please, Mr. Paddington, go right ahead, we'll be fine."

Sam Paddington walked out from behind the counter and led Kyle and Linda to the side, as away from the crowd as they could get, which was not far.

"I feel so terrible," Sam said once they were clustered in a corner. "I keep thinking, if I hadn't canceled on Vic …"

"So you did cancel," Kyle said. "The bartender at Cargill's didn't know. He just said you never showed up."

Sam looked aghast. "Of course I canceled! I would never just stand someone up, and certainly not a friend like Vic. I texted him saying I wasn't feeling well and I was going home early."

Kyle looked at him carefully. "But you feel fine now."

"It's been three days. I would hope I felt better by now. What are you getting at?"

"Nothing, Mr. Paddington, I'm just thinking out loud."

"Monday afternoon I was feeling ... I don't know, food poisoning, but not that bad. Just an upset stomach, and I went home to my apartment in the Village."

"And that was it?" Linda asked.

"That was it."

"Did Vic text you back?"

"Yes, yes he did. He said he was going to buy a suit."

Vincent Campagna had told them the same thing, that his brother wanted a new suit for their niece's christening.

"Here," Sam said, taking his phone off his belt holster. "I still have it."

He went to his message screen, scrolled to Vic Campagna's name and held the phone out for Kyle to see.

No probs. Feel better. Headed to Keller and Whitman for a suit. Want the best for the baby. Call me later.

Sam's face darkened. "I never called him. I feel so terrible."

"You had no way of knowing," Linda said.

"Still ... it would have been nice to hear his voice one last time, before .... before ..."

"What is Keller and Whitman?" Kyle asked, not wanting to lose the thread of their conversation.

"It's a high-end men's store, clothing store, on the Upper East Side. I told Vic he shouldn't spend that kind of money, it's not like he'd be wearing the suit again any time soon. But he insisted, it was a big deal in the family."

Sam put his phone back on his belt. His hand was shaking slightly and Kyle realized how upsetting this was for him.

"Thank you, Mr. Paddington, you've been very helpful."

"Have I?"

"Yes, you have. We'll let you get back to your job now."

"Are you going to see the museum? You paid full price, not everybody does. I've had people pay a dollar. Seriously."

"We'd love to," Kyle said. "Linda's never been here and I'm sure she'd like to spend a day walking around the exhibits, but we just don't have time."

They waved goodbye to Sam Paddington as Kyle led them back out onto the front steps. As they descended, he said, "Something happened."

"Yeah, he got killed!"

"No, I mean something happened either before he got to this Keller and Whitman store, or after he left."

"Maybe something happened *at* the store."

"Right," Kyle said, a little too dismissively. "He goes into a fitting room and runs into the Pride Killer. I doubt that."

"I'm just offering ideas, Kyle. Something to think about."

"Good, really. We need ideas."

"So are we going there? To the store?"

Kyle led Linda to the taxi line. "Maybe tomorrow," he said. "We have dinner with Danny tonight. It'll give us a chance to think this all through."

"Can we afford to wait?" Linda was worried they could lose their momentum.

"If his pattern holds, his next victim will be Thursday or Friday night. That gives us tomorrow to kick this into high gear. I'll find out when this Keller and Whitman store opens and we'll be first in the door."

They got into a taxi and headed south on Fifth Avenue. No sooner had they pulled away from the curb than the driver began chattering in a low voice. He was not talking to himself.

"You said it's illegal," Linda whispered in the back seat.
"So is jaywalking, and look around you."
Kyle was right. New Yorkers all seemed to do as they please. One in particular was about to do it again.

18

Just as Kyle and Linda were heading home for dinner at the apartment, D was walking into Pianissimo, a piano bar on 46th Street in the Theater District. Pianissimo had been around since the mid-1960s and remained a favorite haunt of locals in the know, as well as a steady flow of tourists looking for real New York flavor. More than a few big names in the cabaret scene had developed their chops standing on its small stage, singing standards and the occasional original song they hoped would become one.

D had never been here. He was careful not to meet his candidates in bars where he would be recognized. Described, okay, if it came to that, but not someone known by name or habit. He'd chosen this place because it was on the west side, in a busy area where two men meeting for a drink would blend in with fifty others. He'd also chosen it because he knew it would be quiet, even if someone was at the piano—no video screens here looping dance music clips, no loud pop blaring from suspended speakers—and because it was not a place men their age would stand out. Many of the gay bars in Manhattan catered to a younger crowd and it would be too easy for a bartender or server to remember "the two old guys" sitting at a corner table.

Still, he took his time approaching the bar, looking at his surroundings. He liked to arrive early so he would be in place and he could observe the candidate as he walked in. A lot could be learned from a gait, the way a man carries himself. More than once D had passed on one of them, his instinct telling him this was not a perfect choice and might make the kill difficult. He did not like difficult kills.

He was pleased, then, when he saw Scott walk through the door five minutes late. D had been sitting at a small table along the wall that faced the entrance. He had a glass of white wine in front of him, and when Scott came in looking around at the two dozen customers, D waved at him.

Not bad, he thought, *not bad at all.*

Scott Devlin was fifty-three years old and conscious of his appearance: he was thin, with just a hint of middle-aged paunch. He was middling height, five-nine if one were to guess. He had close-cropped brown hair liberally sprinkled with gray. He was dressed well, in new-looking jeans and a blue-and-white striped shirt covered by a navy sport coat—a little warm for June, but it spoke of a man who wanted to make a good impression.

"Phillip?" he said, walking up to D.

D had accepted at the outset that the only time they would ever know his true name was when they would no longer be able to tell anyone. Sometimes he never did tell them and they died believing he was Phillip or David or Leo.

"Indeed it is," D said. He stood and shook Scott's hand. Firm, he thought, but not too. It was not the handshake of a man he would have trouble overpowering. "And you must be Scott."

"Nice choice," Scott said as he sat at the table. "I've never been here, but it's famous."

"A favorite of mine. I thought you might like it. There's no reason not to, really, and it's quiet enough to talk. That's always a plus."

"I like quiet, too," said Scott. A waiter came over and took his drink order: Scotch and water. A mature man's drink, thought D as he settled back into his chair.

"So tell me about yourself," D said, knowing everything he was about to hear might be a lie.

"Well, I'm between jobs right now. I don't consider myself unemployed, just in transition. It's all in the attitude."

"And what do you do? When you're not in transition."

"I'm a bookkeeper. I worked for the last eleven years at a large bakery in Long Island City that just closed down."

"I'm sorry."

"Don't be. It happens. At least I wasn't the only one let go. We all were."

"And where do you live?"

"I thought I mentioned that in my email."

"You probably did," D said. "My apologies."

"No need," said Scott, eyeing D and smiling. "A man as attractive as you must get quite a few responses."

D feigned embarrassment, shrugging. "It's not that at all. I just don't remember as well as I used to."

"You don't look old enough to be forgetting things yet."

"Call it early onset Chardonnay."

Scott laughed just as his drink arrived. He thanked the waiter and took a sip. "I live in Washington Heights."

"Quite a long subway ride."

"I'm used to it. And what do you do, Phillip?"

D hesitated.

"Are you in transition, too?" Phillip asked, sensing D's reluctance.

"No, not at all. I work with the dying."

Phillip was surprised. "Hospice?"

"Something like that."

D sipped his wine. He'd only had half a glass and intended to keep it that way.

"Listen," D said, "I was wondering if we could have a proper conversation over dinner tomorrow night."

"So I passed the test," Scott said. "I'm impressed … that you're impressed! I'd love to have dinner, but I have plans tomorrow."

D was not happy with the information. He didn't want to have to start over, look for another candidate in such a hurry. Hurrying invites miscalculations.

"But I'm free tonight."

Free tonight, D thought. *That changes things without really changing them. It's not the schedule I had, the plans I'd made, but it will do.*

"Unless you're not, of course, and I would completely understand. There's always next week."

"No, no," D said, "next week is a week too long. I was only planning to finish up some work at home tonight. But if you'll indulge me an hour or so we can just stop there. I have magazines and books you can read, or watch the evening news if you like. I'll wrap things up and we can have a lovely dinner this evening. It just might be the dinner of a lifetime."

Scott was obviously pleased. He smiled and waved at the waiter, about to order another drink.

"Hold off on that," D said. "Let's have a second drink at my townhouse. I have Scotch that's been sealed and waiting for you for seventy-five years."

"Seventy-five-year-old Scotch? You really shouldn't."

"Please, that's what it's for. I've been saving it for a special occasion, and something tells me that occasion has arrived."

D let his leg slide against Scott's under the table. Scott pressed back and a moment later D felt Scott's hand resting on his knee. *How easy they are,* he thought. *How easy.*

The waiter came over, expecting to fill another drink order. Instead, D said to him, "Check please," as he took out his wallet. Scott reached for his and D said, "This one's on me. Now think of where you'd like to have dinner and we'll decide in the taxi."

Scott couldn't believe his good fortune. Meeting Phillip had relieved him for an evening of his worries. No thoughts of being in "transition," no thoughts of dipping into his savings for months as he looked for another job, no thoughts of yet another night alone as so very many of his nights had been. He was feeling especially lucky as they stepped outside and Phillip raised a hand to flag a cab. Soon he would be sipping on Scotch that had waited seventy-five years for him to taste it! It was going to be an evening to remember.

19

It had been a long day for Danny, filled with more emotion than he was used to or would like. Nostalgia wasn't a weakness of his, but he'd spent the afternoon immersed in it: nostalgia for the years he'd been at Margaret's Passion, *with* Margaret. Nostalgia for a time in his life he knew was passing quickly into memory. Nostalgia, even, for the years he knew he could never get back. Time, Danny had learned, was a non-renewable resource, and the older we get, the less of it we have. Unlike anything else in our lives we cannot replace it. It left him with a sense of self-pity, and that was something he disliked in anyone, especially himself.

He was relieved to be at home, back in the apartment with their cats Smelly and Leonard, back with Kyle and their friend Linda. As he prepared the beet and goat cheese salad he reminded himself there were always people with something to truly be sad about. Linda's wife Kirsten was in Phoenix awaiting her arrival while she tended her mother in the final stage of her life. They'd both liked Dot when they met her at the women's wedding. She'd seemed robust enough at the time, but Danny knew cancer could come fast and furious, zero-to-sixty in a matter of months, and that's what had happened to Dot. According to Linda she wasn't expected to live out the month of July and Danny had already spoken to Kyle about going to the funeral if they were invited.

"I love scallops," Linda said. She was standing in the kitchen doorway watching Danny and Kyle prepare dinner.

"The trick is to not overcook them," Kyle said. Frying the scallops was his task and he watched them carefully in the pan, making sure they didn't turn to rubber.

The dinner consisted of scallops, sautéed spinach, baked potato and the salad. It was a rare treat for the men to have dinner at home with a guest. They ate at home often enough, but seldom with anyone else in attendance. It gave Kyle a chance to take out the small folding table they used for company and set it for three. Normally, he and Danny ate sitting on the couch in front of the television, or sometimes on bed trays while they watched something they'd recorded. Smelly and Leonard, too, were delighted to have a visitor. The activity interested them and they kept walking in and out of the kitchen, waiting for something to happen. Smelly was hoping for a scrap of some kind, which she would not get. Leonard, meanwhile, kept marking Linda's ankles with his teeth, sliding them against her as he walked back and forth.

Fifteen minutes later they were all seated at the table. Kyle placed it by the window overlooking Lexington Avenue. It wasn't all that scenic—the view was out over the avenue, and across the street they could see Baruch College. Street sounds drifted up, the occasional car horn, a shout now and then. Kyle hoped they could make it through dinner without the shrill interruption of a siren.

"So how's the party planning going?" Kyle asked Danny, referring to Margaret's going-away celebration.

"It's going fine," Danny said. "I'm just glad it's not a surprise. You can't keep something like this a surprise. Speaking of which …"

Kyle waited a moment for Danny to finish. When he didn't, Kyle said, "Yes? Speaking of surprises?"

"She gave us the building."

Kyle didn't understand. "What do you mean, 'gave us' the building?"

"As in ownership, Kyle. She signed the building over to us."

"That's amazing!" Linda said.

"In good ways and bad," said Danny.

"I still don't understand."

"It's pretty self-explanatory, Kyle. She gave us the deed to the building. Well, to me, but that's the same thing."

Kyle was stunned. They owned their apartment free and clear, but an entire building? What would they do with something like that?

Danny continued: "She said she doesn't need the money, she has that from the restaurant purchase. She can't take the building with her—her words—and she just ... I don't know ... *gave* us the building. Not sold us, not loaned us. Gave us."

"Oh my God," said Kyle. "What are we going to do with it?"

Danny looked at him. "We're going to become landlords, that's what. We're going to keep the restaurant open, and decide what to do with the building twenty years from now."

"Jesus." Kyle's mind was racing. He'd been worried Imogene might take a job in another city and leave him. He didn't want to work for someone else, didn't want to work in an office at all if it came to that. He'd wondered a hundred times what he would do if he lost his job. His photography was a pastime, not a profession. He was weary of being an assistant in his 50s. And now this—a landlord, a restaurateur. Maybe this was the path he was meant to take.

"This is a lot to think about," Kyle said.

"A lot," Danny replied. "But not right now. It was a long day. I've got a party to finish planning, a building to own, whatever that entails. So damn much. And I want a new suit, for Margaret's going-away."

"You've got plenty of suits," Kyle said.

"No. I want something new, something really expensive. Margaret deserves the absolute best, and I'll give that to her."

"You have a tuxedo."

"I don't want a tuxedo. I want Armani, or Versace, something stunning."

The subject of a new suit made Kyle remember the places he and Linda had been that day, the people they'd talked to. "I'm not sure where to start tomorrow," he said to Linda.

"I thought we were going to Keller and Whitman. That seems to be a vanishing point for Victor Campagna."

"What's Keller and Whitman?" Danny asked.

"It's a high-end men's clothing store," Kyle said. "I'm sure they sell some very fine suits. Would you like to go with us?"

"I can't. I've got an appointment in the morning with a florist for centerpieces. Then I have to help Chloe get out invitations. We should have mailed them a week ago. I think I was putting it off, you know, avoiding the whole thing."

"Well," said Kyle, "if we see any suits I think you'd like I'll take some pictures and email them to you." Then, thinking of the surprise Danny had dropped on them at dinner, he said, "A landlord. What the hell? We'll be like Fred and Ethel Mertz without a Lucy and Ricky. Maybe Linda and Kirsten would want to move in. I heard Linda does a mean Babalu."

"No, thank you," Linda said. "I like my little house in the woods, and Kirsten's gotten to like it quite a bit, too. Keep Manhattan, just give me that countryside."

"The parade Sunday might change your mind," said Danny. "It's not like anything you've seen before. The biggest party New York City throws every year."

"I won't change my mind, but thank you. I like New York City as a great place to visit. Let's keep it that way. I'm good for one big parade a year, in someone else's hometown."

Someone else's hometown. It made Kyle think about bodies in the river, the Pride Killer's return. New York City was the killer's hometown, too. He would have to put aside thoughts of owning a building, being a landlord and running Margaret's Passion. Somewhere out there was another man about to be lured to his death unless they moved quickly. He planned to be out of the apartment with Linda first thing in the morning, getting breakfast somewhere as they headed east to be first through the door at Keller and

Whitman. He hoped whoever worked there would remember the young man who came in Monday looking for a suit, assuming he'd made it that far.

20

D didn't like changes to his plans, least of all sudden ones. But what had really changed except the timing? He was careful to always be prepared. There was nothing he was going to do tomorrow night that he couldn't do tonight. And besides, it was too late, unless he wanted to call the whole thing off, and that was out of the question.

He let Scott babble on about looking for a new job, keeping his chin up, refusing to surrender to all the naysaying about the job market and older workers. He smiled and pretended to listen, nodding when he detected a pause, meanwhile having a conversation with himself in the privacy of his mind. Doubt had begun to seep in, and that was entirely new. He wondered if the time had come to stop, to make this his last Pride weekend killing spree and remain forever uncaught. He could become a legend—or more of one than he already was. He could become the most famous serial killer of them all ... the one that got away. He had to consider it. He'd made the foolish mistake of choosing Victor Someone from among his customers. Then he'd hailed a taxi in front of Pianissimo's, instead of walking Scott a block or two to keep from being seen outside the bar. What other mistakes might he make if he kept this up? He knew they weren't deliberate. He was not one of those sad sociopaths who wanted to be caught, to find themselves the subject of tabloid television segments, interviewed from death row. He assumed it was because he'd been out of the game for three years, but was it really a game he wanted to see to its conclusion?

He was deciding to have one last go of it and retire when he glanced out the window at a street sign. 78th Street, three blocks from his home. Better to get out now in case the police somehow found this taxi driver and the man remembered them.

"You can let us off here," D said, leaning forward to speak through the partition.

The cab pulled over. "I've got it," D said, taking a twenty dollar bill out of his wallet and handing it to the driver. He threw the door open and stepped out, not waiting for change.

"This is where you live?" Scott said, looking up at the apartment buildings.

"A couple blocks," D said. "It's such a nice night, let's get some air."

Scott was amendable to a short stroll and the two of them headed up Third Avenue. Five minutes later they turned onto 82nd Street and D led them to his townhouse.

"Upstairs or downstairs?" Scott asked, looking at the four story building in front of them.

"Oh, all of it," D replied, smiling. He could tell by the impressed expression on Scott's face that the seduction had begun. How easily people let down their guard in the presence of wealth, he thought, walking up the four front steps and letting them into his home.

Once they entered they stood in the front entryway, a long hall with dark wood floor planks as old as the house itself. D tossed his keys on an antique crescent table, above which hung a portrait of an elegant woman in a blue gown and raven hair sitting in a red high-backed chair. D had no idea who she was. "My grandmother," he said, nodding at the picture.

Judging by the wealth displayed in the painting, Scott decided money ran in the family and that he'd done quite well on this date. Very different from the last few he'd had. The men he met online were either older and still using profile photos from ten years ago, or younger and disappointed in him for a variety of reasons. He had all but given up dating, and was now glad he'd given it one more chance.

D led them into the living room, which might properly be called a sitting room. There was a television tastefully concealed in an oak cabinet. Along one wall was a fireplace with another portrait above it, this one of a gentleman from the late 1900s and a large dog at his feet. Another stranger D had been looking at for a decade and telling people he was related to.

"This is an amazing house," Scott said. He was afraid to sit on the couch, which looked well-kept but old and expensive.

D saw his hesitation. "Go ahead," he said. "It's made for sitting."

Scott eased down onto the couch, marveling at its softness. Was it velvet? He wasn't sure, and he ran his hand across the fabric. So soft.

D walked over and stood in front of Scott. He cocked his head slightly, curious at this specimen. Scott reached out and placed his hand on D's thigh. A handsome man indeed, thought D. Such a shame. Or such a prize.

D leaned down and kissed Scott. Not passionately, but enticingly. Just a taste.

"What can I get you to drink?" D said. Then, "Oh, wait, Scotch! Scotch for Scott!"

Scott laughed. He was feeling luckier by the minute.

"I happen to have that very old, unopened bottle. No ice, of course. One does not dilute seventy-five-year-old Scotch. I'll be right back."

Scott leaned back against the couch cushion. He watched D turn a corner into a dining room. He began to hum a song to himself, one among his few favorite love songs.

D stopped smiling the moment he turned into the dining room and was out of Scott's line of vision. He walked to his liquor cabinet, another antique he had no use for except as a prop. He leaned down and opened the door, looking into the bottles of rum, Brandy, Bombay Gin and Dewar's. It was not seventy-five years old, but he seriously doubted Scott would know. If he could tell the difference, he wouldn't have long to comment on it. D reached behind the bottles, into the back of the cabinet, and wrapped his hand around the bottle of Rohypnol. One of those and Scott would soon think any Scotch was the best in the world.

Rohypnol acts very quickly. Once Scott began to enjoy his Scotch, commenting on its remarkable flavor, which made D smile, there wasn't much time to get him downstairs.

"I have a wine cellar second to none," D said, watching Scott for any signs of fatigue. It would be coming soon. "At least not second to any I've seen."

"Very nice," Scott replied.

And? D thought. He wasn't expecting a dismissive "very nice."

"I'm not a wine drinker, definitely not a connoisseur."

"I'd still like to show you. It's not something you'll find in most homes, a world-class wine cellar. Come, we'll only be a minute. I imagine you're getting hungry and we should head out."

"I thought you had some work to do."

"I've decided it can wait. Dinner with such a nice gentleman has pushed any thoughts of work right out of my head."

"Well, I was hungry," Scott said. "Now I'm a little woozy."

"Seventy-five year old Scotch will do that to you. Now please, indulge me. I don't often have the pleasure of showing off my wines! You can bring your drink. Better yet, finish it and we'll take a quick trip downstairs."

Scott nodded, then tipped his glass back and drained the rest of the Scotch. He set his glass down on the coffee table, stood unsteadily and followed D toward a door just off the kitchen.

D opened the door. A waft of cool air rushed up at them. It was a welcome sensation for Scott. He was beginning to feel warm, helped by the June weather. Soon it would be hot in New York City, hot and sticky.

"After you," D said, standing aside and motioning down the stairs.

"I don't feel well," Scott said. "I normally hold my liquor quite well. Very strange. You'd think there was something in it …"

A look of dawning realization came over Scott's face. He was on the third step down when he turned back and stared at D, who was no longer smiling.

"What brand of Scotch did you say that was?"

"My own," D said. He stepped forward and with both hands shoved Scott down the stairs. He would not normally do this, but he knew Scott was growing suspicious and he had to act quickly. He did not want to break Scott's neck in a fall—that would ruin the fun—but neither could he risk a struggle.

"Hey!" Scott shouted just as he tumbled backward, down two steps, three, six, finally landing at the bottom of the stairs. His legs felt like rubber and when he flung his hands out grasping for the hand railing, the steps, anything to give him balance and stop his head from swimming, they simply flailed.

"What are you doing?" he managed, looking back up the stairs at D and trying to focus his vision.

D said nothing. The time for explanations had passed—and he never explained himself anyway. He bounded down the steps, leaping the last two over Scott and landing on the basement floor in front of him.

"Help!" Scott cried.

"No one can hear you," D said. "Not your calls for help. Not your screams when they come."

D grabbed Scott's collar and began to drag the now-helpless man across the cellar floor, into his special room. There was an examination table waiting, handcuffs, a state of the art Nikon on a tripod, and the special belt he used to strangle his victims when he was finally done with them. Sometimes it was twenty minutes, sometimes an hour. It all depended how exciting it was and how unwilling they were to have their deaths prolonged. The less they fought, the less he was interested. It was a paradox of the trade: a serial killer who only enjoys the ones who make it hardest to be killed! The easily defeated ones, the ones who went limp or imagined they would please him with passivity, were quickly disposed of. He liked them trying to shout, to call out hopelessly and strain against the bindings. He especially liked the ones who threatened him and told him what they would do to him once they were free. Freedom never came, only a last breath, an exhale of complete surrender. No one would hear that, either. No one except D himself, when he leaned down close, closer, listening to them as they gasped their final breaths.

"I can't hear you," D would say, turning his ear to their mouths. "You'll have to speak up."

He felt the old passion return as he managed to get Scott on the table and begin his inspection. Very nice specimen. He liked them in shape. Age was not a determining factor, and Scott had taken good care of himself.

D began to take his own clothes off. There was seldom much blood; he simply liked to look at himself as he went about his favorite pastime.

He bound Scott to the table, sorry the man was now unconscious. He would have to wake him up when the time came. He didn't go through all this to miss the best part.

The body slipped easily into the East River. They always did, giving out just a splash as they broke the water's surface. D got them there in his car. It's the only reason he kept one in the City. No one really needs a car in Manhattan, unless it's for leaving. D chuckled as he headed back to his Lincoln. He supposed the car *was* for leaving, but he was not the one heading off. It was men like Scott, and Victor Someone, and Kerry and Rafael. He didn't remember all their names. He didn't need to. The souvenirs brought their names back to him. He always kept something, and when he took them out of his bedroom safe he suddenly remembered each and every one in detail.

He reached into his pocket, whistling lightly as he walked. There, next to his own keys, was the set he took from Scott. Just a half dozen keys, to a half dozen locks Scott would never open again. One of them, D knew, was to the man's apartment. It was silent now, as silent as the night. It was a silence that would never be broken again by the sound of the apartment owner walking through the door.

Scott had proven especially defiant. It was a nice surprise; D had expected him to be one of his more pliable victims. He couldn't say why; perhaps he'd let old stereotypes color his perception. But he had been wrong—delightfully wrong—as he'd discovered once Scott regained consciousness. It had tuned into a shouting match with only one of them shouting! No pleading, that was good, he didn't like the simpering ones. Plenty of struggle, with Scott thrashing this way and that, calling for help, his face so red D had feared a stroke might steal the moment from him. But fortune had been on his side once again and Scott had reminded him in every sensual, psychological, physical and emotional way, why he loved what he did so much. It had been both sublime and ecstatic. The only disappointment for the nearly ninety minutes he enjoyed with Scott was that it ended.

He felt fine as he walked to his car. Great, really. He was back in fit form. It had all gone fantastically. He would have to rethink this whole retirement business. Who retires anymore?

21

Kyle had slept fitfully. The dinner had been lovely, followed by a walk around Gramercy Park and down to Union Square. He and Danny wanted to make sure Detective Linda saw plenty of sights on this trip. She hadn't come with a list of things to see and Kyle had not suggested one. He thought the best way to experience New York City was to just show up and go where your interests took you. Their visit to the Met had been ridiculously brief and Kyle meant to ask Linda if she'd like to go back and spend an afternoon there. They only had a few more days—her flight to Phoenix was scheduled for Monday morning. And before that there was the parade Sunday. So little time.

He'd tossed and turned most of the night, disturbed by dreams. In one he was jogging along the East River under a full moon. Jogging was something Kyle would only do in a dream. As he ran along he came upon a small child, a little girl in a frilly yellow church dress, pointing at the water's edge. She said nothing to him, he said nothing to her. Instead he stopped jogging and walked over to the riverbank. There, floating face up, was Danny. Wearing the same clothes he'd had on last night for their walk. Kyle stood staring down into the water, unable to scream, unable to speak. And then, floating into view, coming to rest next to his husband and best friend of nearly eight years, was Detective Linda. Face up, eyes dead, bloated.

Kyle had bolted up from the dream, sucking in his breath. He'd reached down to feel for Smelly, who always slept between them. She was there. Danny was there. They were in bed. The clock read 3:00 a.m. It was only a dream. He'd managed to fall back asleep after telling Danny, who'd woken from the sudden movement, that everything was fine. It took an hour, but the last time Kyle glanced at the clock it was just turning 4:00 a.m.. A moment later he was back asleep, this time dreaming about cats, hundreds of cats in a house of rooms.

He finally got up as the sun began to blanket the sky with early morning light. He quietly went to the kitchen and made coffee for himself. Cup in hand, he padded quietly back to bed in his slippers, tossed them off and slid back onto the mattress. He turned the morning news on low. He knew Danny was awake, but it was one of their differences: Kyle could not stay on his back, staring at the ceiling, or on his side looking out into the dark room. Once his mind clicked on he had to move, even if he just got up for coffee and came back to bed. Danny, on the other hand, had no trouble staying put for another half hour or more.

The familiar faces of Channel 2 filled the TV screen. Kyle had imagined for years that the TV news people were his extended family. He'd had a crush on several of them—the weatherman from Channel 4, and an anchor named George from Channel 7 who had mysteriously vanished three years ago, surfacing in a much smaller market (Kyle kept tabs on them now that the internet made anonymity nearly impossible). He was watching, sipping his coffee, when a "BREAKING" segment came on. A young Asian woman, new to the channel, was reporting live from the East River.

Kyle immediately felt sick. He kept watching.

The name "Melissa Pang" appeared in the left corner, identifying the reporter.

"… the dead man has been identified as Scott Devlin. The information we have so far is that an early morning jogger noticed the body floating near the riverbank around 4:00 a.m. this morning.

The jogger, whose name has not been released, immediately called police."

"Oh my God."

"What?" said Danny, sitting up to watch the news report.

"We made a mistake. A terrible mistake."

"What are you talking about?"

"Shhh!"

Kyle leaned in, focusing his attention on the reporter's words.

"Authorities refuse to say if this is the work of the Pride Killer until further determinations can be made," Melissa said.

"Of course it is!" Kyle shouted at the TV.

"That man was never caught and was believed to have died or left the area, but fear is beginning to spread in New York's gay community. As of this morning, the hashtag #PrideKiller has been trending on Twitter. Can social media solve what the NYPD has failed to for seven years?"

"Great," Danny grumbled. "Everything's a hashtag now."

"I wonder what he kept," Kyle wondered aloud.

"What?"

"A souvenir. The Pride Killer always keeps one."

"And you know this how?"

"They did a profile on him the last time, it was on NYNow. They were getting desperate, hoping to jog someone's memory in the public—and then he stopped. Or went away, or got bored, who knows. But he kept something from all his victims."

"Well, they're not going to tell you what he kept, if they even know," Danny said. "They hold that information back, in case they have a suspect."

"I have to tell Linda."

"Let her sleep, you can't do anything about it at this hour."

"No, she'll want to know."

"I'm already up," Linda said. She was standing in the open doorway, her brown bathrobe held closed with its belt. "I saw it, too."

There was a television in the spare room. Kyle watched sometimes when he was at his desk, and it provided company with something to watch if they wanted to be alone.

"We should have gone."

"Where, Kyle?" Linda said. "Where should we have gone? What should we have done? This isn't your fault. You had no way of knowing."

"But I did. I knew he kills in threes. I knew the second was coming, but not so soon."

Kyle hopped out of bed, sliding his feet back into his slippers.

"Where are you going?" Danny asked. He was up now, too. Luxuriating in bed was not to be his this morning.

"More coffee, and a plan of some kind. We have to move quickly."

Kyle walked past Linda and headed to the kitchen. She turned and followed him, with Smelly and Leonard bounding off the bed and giving chase.

Kyle popped another single serving cup into the machine. "What kind do you want? We have a selection."

Linda stepped past him and looked at the coffee carousel on the counter, deciding between dark Columbian roast and vanilla hazelnut.

"We need to go to that store," Kyle said.

"Keller and Whitman?"

"Yes. Vic Campagna either never made it there, or he left and met his killer shortly after. Maybe he said something to the staff, gave some indication where he was going."

"It's quarter after six in the morning," Linda said. She handed him the vanilla hazelnut pod.

"Yes, I know what time it is, and I want to be there the minute they open. In the meantime I want to watch the news, see if they come out with anything more. And I want to go online. Whoever this Scott Devlin is, he may have a website, or a profile. The more we know before we leave here, the sooner we might have some idea where to look next."

Linda stood quietly, letting Smelly circle her feet. She thought of the gun she'd brought with her, tucked in her suitcase. It had been her father's gun, the one he'd left at home when he went to the store all those years ago and was gunned down outside a corner market in a botched robbery. It was his service pistol from his time as Military Police in Vietnam, a Colt .45 Series 70 government model he'd used as a Cincinnati cop. Her mother gave it to her when she joined the New Hope Police Force but she had never carried it on duty. It was too special for that. She had had kept it, cleaned it, and fired it hundreds of times at a local range, and now that she was retired it was her protection. She did not travel without it—or her permit to carry it as a retired police officer—unless she was flying. At some point soon she would need to let Kyle know she had it, especially now that she intended to bring it with her. She had not believed in putting her safety in anyone's hands but her own since she was eight years old and learned it could be fatal.

22

D ran his fingers over the keys for the hundredth time, feeling the metal with his fingertips, remembering the look of terror in Scott Devlin's eyes as he realized he was dying at the hands of such a refined man, a man of taste who kept seventy-five-year-old Scotch and a Class A wine cellar in his basement. Meeting strangers had always been a gamble, but nothing about D made anyone think he was the least bit dangerous. That was part of the thrill, really. Appearing to be someone so completely different from who he really was. And then, near the end, revealing himself. Surprise! How's that for failing to expect the unexpected!

He was lying in bed, propped up on pillows against the headboard, with his favorite bamboo bed tray across his lap. He'd made his morning tea and accompanied it with buttered toast—a special treat on a special morning. He looked at the clock: 6:00 a.m. The news came on and he watched as the same reporter told the same breaking news that Kyle and Linda were watching on the other side of town. A body had been found in the East River. Speculation was rampant. Something about a hashtag. My, D thought, that was fast. Was it a good sign? A bad sign? No sign at all?

He liked this young reporter; she was a rising star in the local TV news market and he would keep an eye on her, perhaps send her flowers when this was over and he disappeared for another year. He would be back, he had decided that. Retirement was not for him. The uneasiness he'd had after killing Victor Someone and feeling so little fulfillment had subsided. Scott reminded him how good he was at it, how much it meant to him. No, he was not going away, just taking his usual long vacation. But first, there was the spree to finish. The Pride Killer—and by day's end everyone would be saying he'd come home to kill again—made his kills in threes. Three men. Three trips to the basement. Three bodies in the river.

There had to be one more, and as D remembered it clearly now, the third time was the charm. In fact, the hardest part of his yearly ritual was stopping! He made it to three, he enjoyed the escalating pleasure of each kill, and then, on Sunday, he went to the parade. Hundreds of thousands of proud gay men, lesbians, allies, all letters of that ever-expanding acronym marching and hooting and hollering their way down Fifth Avenue. And D, there on a corner, so very proud himself. He belonged to them, and they certainly belonged to him. Thank you, Papa, he thought, nibbling at his toast. Thank you for the photographs and the letters I never answered. Thank you for showing me there is a different way, a better way.

He had decided to find his third victim in a different way as well. The police would be stepping up their efforts. It did not serve the New York City tourism business to have the country's most successful serial killer back in action during one of the biggest celebrations of the year. They would be looking at postings on websites, men seeking men for all sorts of things. And nowadays everything was spied on, everything was filtered. He wanted to do what they would least expect and find his next candidate offline. Someone he met in his everyday life, as long as it was nowhere near the store. He hadn't cruised in a very long time, except twice his first year in Berlin when he was lonely and his mother, demented and taking much too long to die, had become insufferable. It had been more to get out of the house, away from her and the string of aides she hired and fired. He'd gone home with the men and talked, then fooled around just enough to frustrate them before heading back to the dreary reality of a dying mother.

He would cruise again, finding his third victim on a park path or in a Chelsea coffee shop. There were still plenty of gay men in Chelsea among the baby strollers and nannies. He could meet one there. Or maybe the Met or the Guggenheim! Museums were especially fun to cruise in, pretending to look at paintings and sculpture while you were really stealing glances at men doing exactly the same thing!

Whoever he met, and however he met him, it would need to be soon. He'd had to push up his schedule with Scott. The benefit of it was that it gave him more time. He did not have to rush now.

He finished half his toast, leaving the second piece on the plate as he watched the weather forecast for the next five days. It was going to be a perfect weekend. He would excuse himself that afternoon, telling Jarrod, who was coming in late this morning after a doctor's appointment, that he wanted to visit the church where his mother had loved to pray. He would light a votive candle and drop some money in the offering box. She'd never lived in New York City. There was no church, no favorite pew, no candle. Everything Jarrod knew about his boss was a lie. So he would lie again and wander out … cruise out into the world of Manhattan and see who caught his eye. Did he still have what it takes to seduce a stranger with just a smile and a wink? Why yes, he believed he did.

Perfect weather. Perfect plan. Perfect weekend coming soon. He felt so alive, so renewed, that he took the second piece of toast and ate it after all. Why not? He deserved it, and the world deserved him. It was a match made in hell.

23

Kyle still marveled at how time slowed down the faster you wanted it to move. It was now 8:30 a.m. and they had another ninety minutes before Keller and Whitman opened for business. Kyle had done some online research and found nothing about the store that wasn't on its website. Founded in 1995, Keller and Whitman served an exclusive clientele, and also an older one. The few models on the site were mostly mature white men, with one African-American and one Asian thrown in to give it a veneer of diversity; Kyle suspected the only minorities who shopped there were moguls and bankers from Tokyo, Beijing or the safer parts of Mexico City.

The founders of the store were relatives, one Leo Whitman and his nephew Deidrich Keller III. Neither had a photograph on the "About" page, and there was a brief dedication to Leo, with the years 1944-2003 under his name. Kyle took that to mean Keller was running the store alone now. He would find out soon enough, since he and Linda planned to be the first customers through the door.

"What if Victor Campagna never made it there?" Linda asked. They were sitting on the couch as Danny prepared to leave for Margaret's Passion. It was a part of Danny's daily ritual Kyle rarely got to see, since he would normally be heading to his job by now and Danny usually left later in the morning.

"Then we'll know something—or someone—happened to him between the time he left Cargill's bar and the time he expected to be at the men's store."

"Maybe he met someone there. Another customer, or someone outside the store."

The Pride Killer was not careless; he may be stalking his victims first. For all they knew, Victor had been selected days or even weeks before his murder. It could be that the killer simply bided his time until the right opportunity arose for him to act.

"I've thought about that," Kyle said. "I'm starting to think Victor was followed."

Linda nodded; she'd considered the same thing. "And somehow, somewhere along his path, the killer got him to take a detour."

Danny came into the living room. He was dressed for work in black slacks, a light blue shirt and dark tie. He'd always been meticulous in his work appearance and had become more so since he owned the restaurant. The burdens of ownership were several degrees higher and heavier than simply managing the place, and he wanted to always be prepared for doing business, meeting clients as well as customers, and generally looking like he owned one of the best restaurants in Manhattan.

"I'm heading out now," Danny said. He grabbed a lint roller from several they had on a shelf just inside the kitchen. Cat hair was a constant in their home, and he rolled the latest batch from his pants legs.

"You're leaving early," Kyle said.

"More planning to do."

"How's that all going, by the way?"

"Fine, considering this is the one party I never wanted to have. We're whittling down the list, getting the invitations out. We've only got a month. Some people we knew were invited got a 'Save the Date' email a couple weeks ago. Is your mother coming?"

"No," Kyle said, secretly glad of it. There had been increasing friction between Danny and his mother-in-law since they'd been business partners and Kyle wanted this going-away party to be free of it. Sally might have suggestions for the seating plan, suggestions for the menu, even suggestions for who was being invited. Kyle was relieved she'd be on a cruise with her man-friend Farley somewhere in the Caribbean.

"That's right," Danny said, remembering. "She's taking a cruise. Good for her. Better for me." He put the lint roller back on the shelf. "Margaret suggested, now that we have title to the building, we could get a line of credit and buy your mother out."

Kyle hadn't given any thought to being landlords and didn't want to think about it now. But he liked the idea of buying out his mother. It could relieve a source of stress that had been in their lives the last six months.

"Margaret's a smart woman," Kyle said. "Let's talk seriously about that after her going-away party."

Danny nodded. He walked over to Kyle and kissed him goodbye. "Love you," he said. They always said this to each other when they parted, even when one was simply going across the street for milk. Life was unpredictable. People got hit by cars, they had heart attacks. Better to always say "I love you" and not wish later you had.

Danny leaned down and gave Linda a hug. "Please keep an eye on him," he said. "And yourself. One of these days you two are going to go after a killer who's smarter than you are."

It reminded Linda she needed to tell Kyle she'd brought her gun. She would do that as soon as they were alone. There was something about this killer that put her more on guard than usual.

"We'll be fine," Kyle said. "Safety in numbers."

"I'm not convinced 'two' qualifies for that," Danny said. "Bye everybody, bye cats." He waved at Smelly and Leonard. The cats glanced at him, uninterested, as the door closed.

Kyle looked at his watch. They still had over an hour. "Hungry?" he said.

"I could use some breakfast."

"I know a diner, the Moonrise, not far from where we're going."

"Sounds good." Linda got up from the couch. "Let me get my gun and jacket first."

"Your gun?"

"Well, yes. I've been meaning to tell you about that."

Kyle followed Linda into the guest room as she began to tell him about her father's gun—now her gun—and why she planned on bringing it along.

24

Danny walked slowly along Lexington Avenue, south toward 23rd Street. It was only a six-block walk to Margaret's Passion and one he'd taken a few thousand times in the last eleven years. It was also one he knew he would take only a dozen more times before Margaret Bowman was gone. What then? He would get to the restaurant knowing she was not upstairs. And now it was his building! What would he and Kyle do with it? He needed to speak to the managing agent and see about keeping them on, arranging as seamless a transition as possible from Margaret's ownership to theirs. What of the tenants, too? Danny knew some of them. There was the older couple in the second floor apartment next to Margaret's, and the author who lived on the fourth floor and came in for lunch every Tuesday—a woman in her 50s who wrote a wildly successful series in the Young Adult fiction genre. Gladys Markowitz, although she did not write under that name. Danny was trying to think of her pen name as he turned left at 23rd. Tess Collins? Tess Collier? Something like that. Sold books by the hundreds of thousands to teenagers around the world.

Danny stopped on the corner and looked around him. He was acutely aware of how little attention we pay to our surroundings. New York was just a glaring example of it: everyone stumbled along with smart phones in their hands, ear buds shoved into their ears, or both.

Texting, reading, typing, ignoring everything and everyone around them without realizing they would never, ever, encounter this moment again. He'd been guilty of it himself and had only stopped looking at his phone the last few months. Whatever emails were there could wait until he got to work. He and Kyle watched the morning news in bed every day, that was enough. He didn't need to read the New York Times in miniature as he shuffled along Third Avenue. It could all wait—which was exactly the opposite of how the world lived now. Most people thought *nothing* could wait anymore, not their Facebook updates, not the latest tweet from their favorite celebrity, not the endless stream of "click-bait" trying to grab their attention with headlines that would shame a high school newspaper writer at his most vulgar and juvenile. Danny had a dim view of the culture he found himself living in at fifty-six. Was it age? Or was it simply coming to see it all as flotsam clogging the surface of a sea of emptiness?

He smiled at that one, "a sea of emptiness." What did that even mean? He waved at the old man who ran the shoe repair store near the corner of 23rd and Third. He was surprised the store was still there. Almost everyone around it had gone out of business, replaced by other shops that would last six months, maybe a year or two, then they'd be gone as well. Flow and change.

A lot had changed in Danny Durban's life the last seven years. He was married. He owned a restaurant, and now the building it was in. His second mother, the one he loved as dearly as he loved his own, was about to move to Florida for the last few years of her life. But the shoe repair store was still there! Third Avenue was still there! Smelly and Leonard and Kyle were still there. He straightened up, smiled. The sun was out, the temperature expected to stay below 80. What a beautiful morning. So many beautiful mornings he'd missed, walking with his head down, staring at the tiny screen on his phone. No more. Today, and tomorrow, and the next day, he would look at the world around him. He would take comfort in what had *not* changed. He would cherish it all for every moment it lasted and not fall prey to sorrow, wondering when it would end.

He had a party to plan. He had a life to celebrate—Margaret's and his own. And the lives of his cats, and the lives of everyone he loved. His mother, his father, his sisters, his nieces and nephews, his husband, Detective Linda and Kirsten, the old man in the shoe store and the bus driver and the mail lady. Celebrate all of them, celebrate each step he took as he walked along, celebrate being alive.

Yes, he thought, as Margaret's Passion came into view just a half-block ahead. Time for a new suit—literally and figuratively. Time to be alive.

He reached the restaurant and saw Chloe already there. He waved at her through the window; she waved back. Trebor the bartender was there, too, making everything look fabulous for the coming lunch crowd. He opened the door and just stood there looking around at his restaurant. His Margaret's Passion. He would make sure it always lived up to its name, and he would thank Margaret every day of his life for the passion she inspired in him. No time now for sadness, no time for mourning what had not yet passed. It was time to get to work, and do it with a song.

25

Kyle loved diners. There had always been something about them that gave him comfort. He traced it back to his childhood, when he and his parents would go to breakfast on Saturday mornings in Highland Park, Illinois. The Chicago suburb was Kyle's home until he left for college. His father, Bert Callahan, an architect of some renown, died at his desk in the house—the same desk Kyle now used as his own. It was the only possession of his father's Kyle asked for when his mother moved to Chicago. But the memories of the diners had never faded, and he loved sitting in them, interacting with the waiters and waitresses who came by with coffee and an occasional attitude. He liked the feel of the leatherette booths and the paper placemats with advertisements on them for local businesses. Everything about a diner said *home* for Kyle, and they were a way for him to go there no matter where he was: diners on the road when they traveled, diners near their apartment, diners in other states, other worlds. Like comfort food itself, diners were consistent, reliable and soothing.

They'd taken a booth near the window facing Lexington Avenue. It was just nine-thirty and they were only a few blocks from the men's store. Linda was eating light, a fruit bowl with cereal, while Kyle had a Greek omelet, dry toast, no potatoes. He was now aware of the gun Linda carried in a holster beneath her jacket that would be visible only to the trained eye had she not told him about it. Being a retired detective allowed her to carry her firearm across state lines, provided she also had proof she'd qualified with the weapon in the past twelve months. Linda never failed to qualify.

"So here's where we stand," Kyle said, waving away their waitress who was making the rounds with fresh coffee. "We know Victor Campagna was at Cargill's where he was supposed to meet Sam Paddington, who never showed up."

"Sam's last communication with Vic was a text about going to look for a suit. If there were more we'll never know, since there's no phone."

"At least no phone we know about."

"Maybe the phone was the souvenir. You said the Pride Killer always keeps one."

"That's a distinct possibility. And I would guess, given how careful and successful this guy is, that if the cops have the phone, there's nothing on it that will lead them to him. Otherwise there might not be a second victim—they would have stopped him by now."

Kyle had blamed himself all morning for not finding some way to prevent the latest murder. It was useless guilt and fantasy—there was nothing more they could have done—but it troubled him to know the killer had acted outside his pattern. Did it mean he was escalating? That he was in a hurry for some reason? If that was the case he might be meeting his third victim as they spoke.

"No one ever heard from Victor again once he left Cargill's," Kyle continued. "That means he met the killer either before he got to Keller and Whitman, or very soon after. He was in frequent contact with his brother and I just don't think an entire afternoon would pass without another text, another phone call, something."

"Vinnie said Victor had a habit of turning his phone off."

"A bad habit, as it turns out."

Linda thought about it. "So the store is a turning point. But what if he never showed up there?"

"That's what we're going to find out." Kyle quickly finished half his toast and left the other piece on his plate, along with most of his omelet. He wasn't hungry.

"I wish you hadn't brought the gun," he said.

"It's perfectly legal," Linda replied, self-consciously patting her jacket pocket. She could feel the pistol under the cloth. If diners were comforting to Kyle, her father's Colt .45 was comforting to her. "Or are you one of those people who thinks guns are evil?"

"I didn't say they were evil. They just make me nervous."

"That's because you're never around them, Kyle. I've been around guns my entire life and I'd have to say they make the world a safer place. And there's just something about this Pride Killer that makes me want to be very, very careful."

"Fine, Detective, whatever you say."

"I'm a Republican."

Kyle stared at her a moment, not knowing what one had to do with the other.

"I just needed to come out, that's all. I came out as gay not very long ago, and I don't want to be in any closets. Not with my family, not with my social circle, small at it is, and not with you. And I gotta tell you, Kyle, coming out as Republican when you've got gay friends is very risky."

Kyle was silent a moment, then burst out laughing. "You think this is an issue for me? You think I've never voted for a Republican in my life?" (He hadn't, but would not tell her that.) "Pa-leeze!"

"I didn't know. We've never talked politics."

"Listen," Kyle said, as he motioned to the waitress for a check. "You're an ex-cop. You're a kickass lesbian. I am not surprised in the least that you carry a gun, or that you're a Republican. I would've guessed Libertarian."

It was Linda's turn to laugh. It gave them both a brief reprieve from the seriousness they'd been immersed in the last twenty-four hours.

"Let's just hope your aim is better than your judgment." Kyle winked as he pulled out his wallet. "Breakfast is on me."

Kyle took out several ones and placed them on the table for a tip, then grabbed the check and slid out of the booth. Keller and Whitman was scheduled to open in ten minutes and he had a lot of questions to ask there. A man's life could depend on the answers.

26

D was distracted and wished Jarrod had not had a doctor's appointment. The morning after a kill was always like this, as if he couldn't stop reliving the pleasure and excitement of it: the helplessness and fear in his victim's eyes, the belt around the neck, the indescribable ecstasy of seeing life extinguished like a flame that has burned its last molecule of oxygen. Then the pictures—click, pose, click, pose, some flash, some natural lighting—and the disposal. He even enjoyed that last part, wrapping the body in a plastic sheet, getting it to the river undetected, and dropping it in. Splish splash! Then home, slowly, already savoring the sense memories of the last few hours. And now the morning.

He'd kept Scott Devlin's keys in his right pants pocket. He did that on his mornings-after, bringing his souvenir to work with him. He could feel the keys jangling against his leg. He slid his hand in his pocket, fingering the metal on his skin, the contours. He was seeing it all again, the terrible surprise on Scott's face, when he looked up and saw them through the front window. A man and a tall woman coming into the store. Very early. Of course, when you ran a store, there was no such thing as too early. You wanted customers as soon as the door was unlocked, and here were two of them. He took his hand out of his pocket and smiled at Kyle and Linda as they entered.

"Good morning," D said, stepping out from behind the counter.

"Morning," said Kyle. He'd talked over their approach as they walked from the diner. It would not be a direct questioning, at least not at first. He wanted the chance to see what was here, to get a feel for the place and whoever worked at the store.

Linda went along, following Kyle a few steps behind. Both of them began to look around at the clothes as if they were regular shoppers, or tourists who'd heard of the store's reputation.

"How may I help you?" D said, smiling.

"Not really sure yet," Kyle said. "I'm looking at suits."

D was now standing next to Kyle at a small rack of very high-priced suits.

"Is there an occasion in mind? We could start with your measurements, go with something custom made."

"It's not for me." Kyle ran his fingers over a charcoal gray suit coat. "It's for my partner. He has a special event to attend but he's very busy. I thought I'd look around for him, save him some time."

"I see," said D. He glanced at Linda, who was standing ten feet or so away, appearing to look at a display of ties.

Something wasn't right here. D considered his instincts impeccable and there was something off with these two. Was it the way they appeared *too* casual? And why was the woman keeping her distance, as if she were listening and not really looking?

"What's the event?" D asked. His smile was still there, but the corners of his mouth had fallen slightly.

"A going away party," Kyle said. "He works at Margaret's Passion."

"The restaurant?"

"That's the one."

"I've heard of it, although I've never been there. Is he a maître d?"

"No, he's the owner."

"Oh, pardon me," said D.

"No offense taken," Kyle said. "There's nothing wrong with being a maître d! But no, we own the restaurant."

We. D relaxed slightly. This was indeed a man of means. Margaret's Passion was known as one of the best restaurants in the city. Like Keller and Whitman, its customers came from the upper echelons of Manhattan society. D's suspicion was quickly pushed aside at the thought of selling a most expensive suit—several if he did his best.

"My name's Kyle Callahan, by the way. And this is my sister, Linda." He waved Linda over.

"Good morning," Linda said as she approached the man.

"Very nice to meet you both."

"A friend told us this was the place to buy the best suit in town," Kyle said.

"Really?" said D. "How nice of your friend to speak well of us. We won't disappoint!"

Kyle took out the photograph of Victor Campagna. "Actually, you may know him."

This was the moment of surprise Kyle wanted. He watched D's facial expression, his body language, as he held up the picture.

"He was here three days ago."

D froze, but only on the inside. He remained casual, very careful not to give away any recognition of the photograph.

"No," D said, shaking his head. "I don't know this man. Do you always carry photographs of your friends?"

"Only the dead ones," Linda said.

"I see." D noticed the slight bulge against her jacket and knew there was a gun holster beneath it. "You're with the police?"

"For the most part," said Linda.

Hmm, thought D, *for the most part.* They must be private detectives, or one of them was. Why the charade? To see how he reacted?

"Take another look, please," Kyle said, holding out the photograph again. "He was found in the East River sometime between midnight Monday and early Tuesday morning."

D pretended to look closely, to scan his memory. "No, I'm sorry. Did he say he was here?"

"He said he was coming here."

"I wish I could help you, but I've never seen this man."

Kyle glanced around the store. "Do you work here alone?"

"I own Keller and Whitman," D said. "My name is Deidrich Keller. Mr. Whitman, my uncle, passed away some years ago. And yes, I work alone here, unless I need assistance. I have a part-time worker for busy days but Monday was not one of them. I was alone here all day. This man did not come in."

Kyle hoped his disappointment wasn't visible. He'd seen no indication in Deidrich Keller's reaction that he was lying. Somehow, somewhere along the way, as Victor Campagna traveled from Cargill's bar to this store, he was detoured. But why, and by whom?

"Thank you for your time, Mr. Keller," Kyle said, putting the picture of Victor back in his shirt pocket. He took his wallet out and pulled out a business card from Japan TV3. It listed his name, his title of Personal Assistant to Imogene Landis (she had insisted on this and Kyle still hated it after six years), with his office phone and cell number. He handed it to D. "If anything jogs your memory ..."

"He wasn't here, I'm so sorry."

"Still, if anything comes up, or you hear of anything, please call my cell number."

"Will do," said D. Then, to Linda, "Are you a private detective, by any chance?"

"No," Linda said. "Retired homicide detective, from the New Hope police force."

"Pennsylvania?"

"Yes."

"I've never been to New Hope, but I've heard so many good things about it."

"Visit us sometime, everything you've heard is true. It's a great place."

Kyle and Linda headed for the door. Linda stopped as they were about to leave, turned back to D and said, "Why did you think I was a private detective?"

"I noticed your firearm."

Linda looked surprised.

"I'm a tailor by profession," D said. "I notice everything about a man's clothes. Or a woman's."

"Thank you again for your time," Kyle said. He opened the door and held it for Linda. A moment later they were out on the sidewalk.

D watched them walk south on Lexington Avenue. His smile vanished the moment they were out of sight. How did they know about Victor Campagna coming to the store? Who else knew? He had just been visited by a man tracing the steps of his victim, and a woman who carried a gun. Would they let it go and move on? Or would they come back, forcing him to act? And what exactly would he do if it came to that? Choosing Victor Someone from his customers was a stupid mistake. *Stupid, stupid, stupid mistake,* he thought.

He felt himself sweating despite the coolness in the air-conditioned store. This was bad. Deidrich Kristof Keller III never sweated. He would have to do something about this, he just didn't know yet what that was. He glanced at his watch: 11:00 a.m. Thank God Jarrod had a doctor's appointment that morning. He would be in soon, and D would need to take leave. He wasn't feeling well. Jarrod would understand. Such a good, clueless, devoted man Jarrod was. It would be a shame to kill him. Perhaps D could send him on a surprise vacation somewhere, in appreciation for his years of remarkable service. A sudden, surprise holiday somewhere far away.

If these two found him, the police might not be far away. Time had been on his side all these years. Time had been his friend, but now it was staring him down.

He would not blink.

27

Kyle and Linda walked down a half block from Keller and Whitman. Kyle stopped near the corner and took a seat on a bus bench. It wasn't like any bus bench Linda had seen: a single, curved piece of aluminum with low handles strategically placed to create three seats. Kyle took one end, Linda the other.

"This is a bus bench?" Linda asked, wondering how uncomfortable it must be for anyone who didn't fit between the handles.

"It's the new thing in urban architecture," Kyle said. "You'll notice there's no enclosure, either. When it rains, you get wet. Bus benches designed for comfort and shelter have gone the way of pay phones. Now it's all about the homeless."

Linda looked down at the bench they were sitting on. "The homeless?"

"Think about it."

Linda quickly understood. The benches were impossible to lie on, being both spiked and rounded. Only an infant might be able to lie between seat handles. And the absence of any shelter made them distinctly temporary: you were meant to sit here, if you sat at all, only until the next bus came.

"New York has changed so much since I moved here thirty years ago," Kyle said. "It's for the wealthy now—at least Manhattan is, and good luck finding much affordable in the outer boroughs. They don't want poor people here, and the homeless are treated like pigeons. At least people feed the pigeons, but I think it's against the law. Pretty much everything is."

Linda liked what she'd seen of Manhattan so far and wasn't sure she would prefer it the way it had been. She'd read about the success the city had with Times Square, turning it from a dangerous playground for degenerates and criminals into a place you could bring a family. Was it better then, she wondered. Kyle thought so, but Linda had her doubts.

"What did you think of his story?" Linda asked, referring to Deidrich Keller.

"It wasn't much of a story. He said Victor never came in, and there's no reason to doubt him."

"So where did he go?"

"That's the million dollar question. He was at Cargill's, we know that. He left and headed here but never made it."

"And there was no more communication with anyone after that."

"We don't know that," said Kyle. "We don't have his phone. We don't know if anyone has his phone. The police might have it. The killer might have it."

"Or," said Linda, "he may simply have turned it off, or ignored it. I do that sometimes. I hate a vibrating phone, it's like Pavlov calling to his dog. Vic's brother said he liked to disengage. Anything could have happened that afternoon and evening."

"Correction," Kyle said. "Something did happen. Victor Campagna was killed. But he had to get there, wherever 'there' is. He had to go *somewhere* after he left Cargill's, and the most obvious direction for him to head was here, where he intended to go. I mean, for godsake, it's only six blocks!"

"Did you see the moving *Vanishing?*"

"What?"

"Vanishing," Linda said. "It was about this couple who stop at a gas station. The woman goes inside to buy something and never comes back."

"No, sorry, I didn't."

"Well, we seem to be looking at something like that. My point is that no one simply disappears. There's always somewhere they went, or someone who took them—willingly or not."

They sat in silence another minute. A bus came by and stopped in front of them, letting two people off. Linda gave a small wave to the driver and watched as an elderly woman with a cart on wheels climbed up into the bus and took a seat in front. The bus pulled away.

"Let's walk it," Kyle said.

"Walk where?"

"From Cargill's to here. Let's go back to Cargill's, imagine we're Victor and follow in his footsteps. We have his picture. I say we stop in every store and ask if they saw him, or if they saw him talking to someone."

Linda did a quick calculation in her head. "That's probably thirty stores, on one side of the street. Sixty if we hit both sides."

"We'll be logical about it. We'll go back to Cargill's, which is on the south side of the street. We take an immediate right, which most people would do. We walk up to Lexington, cross to the east side—the side we're on—and head north."

The directions meant nothing to Linda. She knew most of Manhattan was designed in a grid, which made navigating the city very easy once you understood the 'north, south, east, west' business, and the whole 'uptown, downtown' thing. Generally speaking, Fifth Avenue was the dividing line between east and west. She had no idea if there was one for north and south, but she knew if you were going downtown you were going south, and if you were going uptown you were going north. And to know you were going in one of those directions was as easy as looking at the street signs: the numbers only went up or down! Cargill's was near the corner of Lexington and 72nd Street. Keller and Whitman was on Lexington near 78th. Six blocks. Thirty stores.

They stood from the bench. Linda looked at it again, wondering who sat in a room and came up with the idea for bus benches that could only be endured for very short periods of time and could never provide comfort for the homeless or weary. Subtly sadistic. Maybe Kyle was right. Maybe New York was now a place that welcomed only money. She was beginning to be glad she hadn't come here for thirty-five years until last spring. She had no before-and-after comparisons to make. She knew only the magical city she'd been to with her parents when she was eight years old. That was the New York City she had wanted to remember. Now, all these years later, it was its own version of pristine. There was still garbage everywhere, and scaffolding covering what looked like half the buildings. But it did not feel dangerous anymore. Clearly the victims of the Pride Killer found out it still was.

Her hand unconsciously dropped down to pat the gun beneath her jacket. It was an automatic gesture, making sure it was still there, seeking comfort in its bulk and its lethality. Some people sought food for comfort, some sought booze, some sought the embrace of a lover for the night or a lifetime. Linda sought the grip of a Colt .45.

28

D watched from the corner of the store. He'd seen them walk to the bus bench and sit down. He thought they might be going downtown, but then a bus pulled to the curb and they did not get on. They were talking. What were they talking about, he wondered. Were they comparing notes? Were they preparing to come back and ask him more questions?

They had not seen Jarrod enter the store just a few minutes after they'd left. And if they had, they would only think he was another customer. His luck was holding out and he tried to be soothed by it, even as an unfamiliar nervousness took root in him.

Deidrich Kristof Keller III believed himself destined to be remembered as the Pride Killer, among the most successful killers America has ever known. But unlike its most famous celebrity killers, he would not be caught. His murders would go unsolved. He would be the modern Jack the Ripper, as well known as any Hollywood star or politician, and with a reputation far outlasting most.

He had only been questioned once before, after his first victim. He'd met the young man through an advertisement in one of the gay newspapers that were stacked outside the bars. David was his name (a killer remembers his first victim the way he remembers his first love; they may well be the same). He called himself a "body worker" and only did outcalls. D thought at the time David probably lived at home with his parents, or a lover. For whatever reasons, he did not want his clients coming to his home, so he headed off to the Upper East Side to an address D had given him several blocks from his townhouse. When David arrived and was understandably surprised to see the man he knew as Leo waiting for him in front of an abandoned jewelry store, D told him it was a precaution. Body workers were not the only ones who took measures to protect themselves. Come, let's walk, D had said. Tell me about yourself. This way he had a chance to take the measure of this man and to keep him from knowing where he was really going. David might write down the addresses of his customers and D wanted no trail that could lead directly to him.

The questioning had been by accident. Two detectives, frustrated at a lack of progress, had canvassed the area where the cabbie said he'd dropped David off. Despite being several blocks away, they knocked at D's townhouse as they went door to door asking if anyone had seen the young man. No, D told them, he had not seen the man he had recently killed in his basement (leaving out that detail). Perhaps his wife had seen him, but she was gone at the moment with their daughter at an orthodontist appointment. Should he call her? They told him not to trouble her and headed on to the next building. That was as close as D had ever come to being found out, which was not close at all. Until this morning. Until the man and woman came into his store.

"I've seen flyers," Jarrod said. He was behind D, opening a shipment of cufflinks that had arrived late the previous afternoon.

It startled D out of his reverie. He turned around. "Pardon me?"

"Flyers, Mr. K, of that young man they found in the river. I saw several posted around the area."

This was news to D—bad news. It must be the man's family. They'd done it before, several times over the four years he'd been active before going to Berlin. Desperate posters with the faces of missing men and a toll-free number to call. All of them had taken their last breaths as he watched them, their eyes bulging out, their bodies convulsing. He had not seen these latest flyers and was worried now. He may need to think of moving after this. Yes, Keller and Whitman may need to close, the townhouse may need to be sold, and D may need to relocate to another large city. Maybe take a year off, then resume his trade. He would have to think it all through very carefully.

"I'm not feeling well, Jarrod," he said.

"Again? You might want to see a doctor, Mr. K."

"I'll be fine. I just need to go home and rest. I haven't been sleeping well. I'm just tired, really."

"By all means go home and lie down then. I've got the store."

"You always do, Jarrod. I've counted on you for a long time now, and you have never let me down."

D prepared to leave.

"What if someone comes in here asking?" Jarrod said.

"About what?"

"About that young man."

D stared at him. "What young man is that, Jarrod?"

"The one who's missing. The one on the flyers. I'm sure he was in here."

"Oh," said D, in as cold and flat a voice as his assistant had ever heard. "They were already here. I told them the young man had come in looking for a suit but had not seen anything to his liking."

"But I thought …"

"What, Jarrod? What did you think?"

A chill ran through Jarrod that froze his blood. He clearly remembered his boss talking to the young man, and in a very friendly tone. He hadn't heard their conversation, but he could swear the young man, the one whose face was now on flyers being put up around the area, had said, "See you later."

"Nothing," Jarrod said. "Nothing, Mr. K. I'm glad you told them whatever they needed to know. I won't worry about it. Now you just go home and rest. Take the day if you need to, I'll be here till closing."

"That's a good man. I'll call you if I'm coming back."

"No need to call. Just surprise me."

Oh, I'll surprise you, D thought. *When this is over, when it's time for me to quickly and quietly disappear, I'll have a very big surprise for you.*

"See you later then," D said. "Or maybe not. It will be a surprise."

D left the store, looking down the sidewalk as he did to see if the man and woman were still there. They were not.

Jarrod stood behind the counter absent-mindedly fingering the cufflink boxes. For the first time in his years of working for Deidrich Keller he had the sense that he did not know the man at all ... and that he did not want to. Something was not right. He began to hope the police would come by again. He would be a good citizen, even though he knew there was nothing untoward about Mr. K's encounter with the dead man. He may have misheard their conversation. The young man may not have said, "See you later." But he would tell them and let them decide. He was just a sales clerk, a retail assistant. He did what he was told. Mr. K had not told him to *not* say anything. He decided he would pass on what he had heard and seen, *if* they came back. He would not seek them out. He would not call the police, but if they came in asking questions again, he would just politely tell them about Monday afternoon. There would be no harm intended, and surely none caused, but the man's family must be frantic by now to learn anything about his disappearance. Mr. K surely had nothing to do with that, but if Jarrod could help them in their search, then that was his duty.

29

It was nearly noon and Kyle and Linda had managed to cover five blocks, stopping and asking store owners if they had seen Victor Campagna walking by on Monday afternoon. As he had feared, Kyle soon discovered how little attention people paid to each other in their daily routines. Most of the shop staff did not spend much time looking out their windows—they were busy watching the customers who'd come in, offering to help them find what they were looking for, or hovering nearby to make sure they didn't steal anything. They struck out at the dry cleaners, the shoe repair store, two diners, and a newly installed pinball arcade where the machines were for sale as well as play.

"I'm beginning to think he never left the bar," Linda said, as they walked north on Lexington just a block from Keller and Whitman.

"Or he didn't get very far from it." Kyle was disappointed, too, having placed his hopes on a sighting by someone along the avenue.

"Keep in mind it was the afternoon. People pay less attention then. They've been at work all day, they want to go home or out to play. They're thinking of themselves more than they are of passersby."

"True," said Kyle. He was feeling glum. There had already been a second victim, ahead of schedule. For all they knew the third victim was selected and might be heading to his death right now. The thought depressed and angered him. He kept thinking they'd missed something, that if they'd asked a different question at Cargill's, or in any of the businesses they'd stopped in, they could have jogged someone's memory.

"Should we keep going?" Linda asked. "We backtracked. Should we move forward now, stop in all the shops heading uptown?"

"I don't know. I just don't know."

There was a newsstand a half block from Keller and Whitman's. Just a hole in the wall, a narrow box of a shop where the owner sold a dozen newspapers, gum, candy, and sodas from a small back cooler. "Let's stop in here," Kyle said.

"Who reads newspapers anymore?" Linda asked as they entered the small store. She, like everyone she knew, got her news online now. She barely used her smartphone as a phone, except to call Kirsten. "Shit!" she blurted.

"What?" Kyle said, startled.

"I forgot to call Kirsten this morning. Listen, you talk to this guy and I'll wait outside. I call her every day. She'll be wondering what's wrong." She pulled her phone out of her purse. There were two messages in her voicemail. "Too late. She's called me. I had the damn thing on silent mode."

"Go," Kyle said. "I'll meet you outside."

Linda left the store to make her phone call. Kyle walked up to the man seated on a stool behind the counter. He'd watched them when they'd come in but had said nothing.

"No more cigarettes," the man said.

Kyle looked at the wall behind the man and was surprised to see an empty cigarette rack. "I don't smoke," he said.

"Gum? Candy? Not too many newspapers left, they go fast."

"Actually," Kyle said, taking out the photograph of Victor, "I was hoping you may have seen this man. Monday afternoon." He handed the picture to the shop owner. "What's your name, by the way?"

"You first."

"Kyle. Kyle Callahan. I'm trying to find my friend."

"Omar. I'm the owner here, twenty years. Everybody else come and go, but Omar stays."

The man took a pair of glasses from under the counter and perched them on his nose. He stared at the picture. "This is the one they found in the river, yes?"

"Yes, I'm sorry to say."

"Then you found who you are looking for."

Kyle couldn't tell if the man was being facetious or just literal. "Okay, then, I'm trying to find out where he went *before* they found him in the river. He was last known to be in this area."

The man peered again at the picture, then handed it back. Kyle felt his disappointment rising. He expected to hit another dead end among too many that day.

"Sure, I saw him."

"Really?"

The man, who Kyle now knew was named Omar, scowled at him. "What, you think I'm just saying it?"

"No, no, I believe you." Kyle glanced out the window and saw Linda talking on her phone. He wished she was with him to hear this.

"I was outside smoking—I smoke them, I just don't sell them—and I saw him come out of the store."

"Which store is that?"

"The men's store, the snooty one. Their customers never come in here. That's why I notice him. He leaves the men's store and comes in here to buy gum. He speaks to me. Not everybody does. Most just put what they buy on the counter, pay and leave. But this young man, he was very nice."

"What did he say?" asked Kyle.

"He say he's feeling lucky, or it was his lucky day, something like that. Maybe he felt lucky because he didn't buy a suit. Very overpriced, that place, I went there once. My brother's a tailor. You need a suit, I get you a good one at half what you pay there."

"Thank you, Omar. I don't need a suit but I'll keep it in mind."

Omar handed the photograph back. "I'm sorry about your friend," he said. "I guess it wasn't his lucky day after all."

Kyle took the picture and slipped it back in his pocket. He quickly picked out a pack of spearmint gum and tossed a ten dollar bill on the counter. Omar rang up the purchase and was taking out the change when Kyle said, "Keep it," and hurried out of the store.

Linda was saying goodbye as Kyle came out on the sidewalk.

"How's Kirsten and her mother?" Kyle said.

"I can't say fine. Dot's in the final stages, but they're keeping her comfortable. Kirsten thinks we're looking at a week, two at the most."

"I'm so sorry."

"It happens … to all of us. Some people just have the misfortune of dying in pain. My concern is getting Kirsten through this. I didn't tell her about the Pride Killer, that's not something she needs on her mind."

"Right."

"How did it go in there? Nothing helpful?"

"Oh," said Kyle, "to the contrary. It was very helpful. He saw Victor Campagna. They spoke."

"What did they say?"

"Omar didn't say anything, as far as I know. But Victor told him it was his lucky day."

It was an odd thing to tell a stranger, unless you'd just had a nice surprise. "I wonder what he meant by that."

"I don't know, but I know someone who might. Someone who told us he'd never seen Victor."

"Deidrich Keller."

"You guessed it. Omar—that's the store owner—said Victor had just come out of Keller and Whitman. He was there, and something happened that put him in a very good mood."

"I think it's time to pay another visit," Linda said. She slipped her phone back in her purse and the two of them began walking toward the men's store.

Kyle wondered what Deidrich Keller would tell them this time. Whatever it was, he knew it would be a lie.

30

D had never suffered from claustrophobia and could not even define it, other than as the fear of confined spaces. Whatever people afflicted with it experience, he imagined it to be what he was feeling now: confined, boxed in, with the walls seeming to close in on him. He had miscalculated badly. He blamed it on being out of the game for three years—damn his mother! Damn Berlin! He had gotten cocky on his return, assuming his ability to remain not just un-captured, but unsuspected all these years, was the natural order of things. He felt invisible, as if he could simply choose his first victim from any man he met on the street, as if he could say to the world, Look, I am invincible, you see me but you don't! I can do this with impunity. And so he had chatted up Victor Campagna when he came into the store, giving no thought at all to Jarrod observing from the counter or across the room. Giving no thought to Victor leaving any kind of trail, no thought whatsoever to the police following that trail, and certainly no thought to a stranger and his sister coming in to ask questions.

Think, Deidrich, think clearly, he mumbled to himself as he paced his living room. They may have their suspicions, but what could they really know? No one on the police force had come to see him. No questions had been asked, except by the man and woman in the store that morning. There was no *proof*. He was overreacting. He needed to relax. He went to the liquor cabinet and poured himself a small snifter of brandy. Drinking was not something he allowed himself during the day, but his nerves were on edge and he needed to slow down, to relieve the sense that everything was about to come crashing down on him.

He was a world traveler. He had a valid passport, with stamps from a dozen countries. He could always go back to Germany. He'd learned enough of the language to get by for the time it would take to establish a new identity. And while he hated the time he'd spent there, it was just the sort of place he could vanish. He took his snifter to the couch, sat down and enjoyed the warmth of the brandy spreading through him.

A few minutes later he was slumped on the couch, enveloped by the cushions. So comfortable, so comforting. He'd finished his brandy and was contemplating a second glass as he let his memories wash over him. Each of his fourteen victims had sat on this couch. Each had been happy to have met such a nice man, such a refined man, who welcomed them into his home. Each had relaxed as he now relaxed, and soon, after a drink of their own, each had gone to his basement for the biggest, most spectacular and final surprise of their lives.

You knew it had to end sometime, Deidrich, he thought. *Even the best dreams end with the opening of an eye, the dull workaday world coming back into focus as the sweet dream recedes. It won't be long. Do what you need to do, then dream again.*

All would be well, he knew that now. The mind, once calmed, is the most powerful thing on Earth. Everything man has accomplished began in his mind. Every vision made reality, every towering achievement, every work of art. His life was a work of art, he believed that with all his heart. There had never been one like him, and there would never be one like him when he was gone. And he would go. He knew that now, too, in the clear calm of his soothed mind. It was all a fiction anyway, was it not? The townhouse, the paintings, the appearance of a life he'd built here, even the store. All of it had been manufactured to serve his one true purpose, and that was the only thing he lived to fulfill.

He was hungry now. He decided to have just a few more drops of the brandy, then head out for a nice meal. The only thing that eased a troubled soul more than a good stiff drink was fine food. He wanted some. He stood from the couch just a tiny bit unsteadily and headed back to the liquor cabinet. One more taste, one more slow, luscious swallow of the hot powerful liquid, and he would leave the townhouse. He would take a taxi, give the man directions, and head south.

31

Jarrod saw the couple through the store window as they approached the door. The woman was taller than the man and quite striking, with her long hair and her navy jacket. They were deep in conversation and Jarrod wondered what they were talking about. He'd entertained himself for years by making up stories about people he saw, strangers, and the conversations they had with themselves. He imagined they were talking about a wedding they were planning to attend. The man needed a suit for the wedding but hated wearing suits. He did not strike Jarrod, upon first impression and from a distance, as the type who dressed up unless he had to. But weddings were special events, and the woman was telling him he had no choice. This was her brother's wedding—to a man, no less, something that gave Jarrod a special tingle while stirring his own sad longing for love. (He'd thought when he first met Mr. K there might be something there, but he'd been wrong and quickly let it go.)

Kyle and Linda walked into the store and Kyle noticed the man near the counter staring at them as he quickly pasted on his best may-I-help-you smile. It was not Deidrich Keller and Kyle guessed it was his assistant, the one they'd been lead to believe was rarely there. The man looked to be in his 50s, slim and stylishly dressed in dark pants and matching sport coat. He wore a thin gray tie with a small diamond tie-pin at its midpoint. His hair was artificially black, but not the sort of shoe-polish look that some young hipster types wore or that made some older men look ridiculous. Just clearly dyed.

"May I help you?" Jarrod asked.

"We were looking for Deidrich Keller," Kyle said. "We spoke to him earlier and were under the impression he would still be here."

"He didn't mention having help today," Linda added.

Help? Jarrod thought. Is that how they thought of him? Surely Mr. Keller had not referred to him that way. He was an *assistant*. An Assistant Store Manager, if one wanted to rely on titles. But not *help*.

"I'm here every day," Jarrod said. "Perhaps if he referred to the help he meant the cleaning crew that comes in on Sundays. But of course it's not Sunday."

"Of course not," Kyle said. He could tell Linda's comment rubbed the man the wrong way. This could work to his advantage if he made this man annoyed with his boss. "Surely that's what he meant, not you."

"Definitely not."

Kyle extended his hand. "I'm Kyle, by the way. Kyle Callahan, and this is my associate Linda Sikorsky."

Linda nodded, declining to extend her hand. She was remaining silent, waiting to see how Kyle played this.

"Jarrod Sperling. I've been Mr. Keller's assistant here—Assistant Manager, that is—for nearly seven years. I basically run the store when he needs to be out, which is fairly often. Are you looking for a suit? A nice ensemble of some kind?"

"No. We're actually asking around about a friend of mine." Kyle took out the photo of Victor Campagna and showed it to Jarrod.

"Oh, my," Jarrod said, and Kyle knew he recognized Victor. "I've definitely seen him before ... on the news. It's terrible what happened to him. But are they sure he didn't fall into the river? It happens sometimes. People have too much to drink, they get too close to the water's edge."

"That's what we're trying to find out."

"Are you with the police?"

"Yes and no," Linda interjected. "I'm a private detective, hired by Victor's family."

Something was peculiar with these two, Jarrod thought. First they were "associates." Then they were friends of the poor young dead man. Now one of them is a private detective. His guard went up. What should he tell them? And should he tell Mr. K first? Had they been the police it would be different, but they were not. He did not want to do or say something that could get him in trouble. He liked his life, he liked his job, he liked his status as Assistant Manager in one of the city's finest men's clothing boutiques. This was not a boat he wanted to rock.

"Well," he said, "other than on the news reports and the flyers, I can't say I've seen him before." It was a lie and Jarrod could feel his face flush, hoping it was only something he felt and not something they saw.

"We'd like to ask Deidrich a few more questions," Linda said. "Might you have his home address?"

Something was definitely fishy now. What private detective worth her pay could not find someone's home address? And that information was private. Jarrod had never, not once, given our Mr. K's address or his phone number.

"He's at a meeting," Jarrod said.

Kyle: "A meeting?"

"With one of our suppliers."

"Do you know when he'll be back?" asked Linda.

"Um … no, I don't. Sometimes he doesn't come back until the next day. He doesn't need to come back. He has me here."

"Yes, of course," said Kyle, "his Assistant Manager." This had gotten them nowhere, and he believed Jarrod was hiding something.

Linda took out her business card and handed it to Jarrod. It was the card for her vintage store in New Hope that listed her cell phone number.

Jarrod read it and looked at her curiously. "*For Pete's Sake?*" he said, reading the store name.

"It's my cover."

"An undercover private detective. I didn't know there was such a thing."

"Just please call me if Mr. Keller returns. It's very important. The family is distraught and I've promised to do all I can to find out what happened to their son."

"Do you think Mr. K ... Mr. Keller, might know something?"

"That's what we'd like to find out," Kyle said. "Not that he had anything to do with the disappearance, just if he might remember something, anything, about seeing Victor walk by or perhaps stop and look in the window here. Please give us a ring if Mr. Keller returns, it's a simple request."

"Yes, yes, of course."

Kyle and Linda prepared to leave. They both felt they'd been stonewalled and that the first thing Jarrod Sperling would do when they left was call Deidrich Keller. Maybe this was a good thing: having been to his store twice in one day, they might have him on edge, thinking too quickly and ripe for making a costly error.

"By the way," Kyle said as they were about to turn and leave. "You said you ran the store for Deidrich Keller when he wasn't here."

"Yes," Jarrod said, stiffening proudly.

"Did you ever run it for him for an extended period?"

"Why yes, I did. I ran it for him for nearly three years."

Kyle stared at him. He felt as if a shadow had just come over them. "Three years? Really?"

"Mr. Keller spent time in Germany. Berlin, to be exact, taking care of his mother. He's only been back a few months. Why do you ask?"

"No reason," said Kyle. "Thank you for your time. And if you do hear from him, please call that cell phone number on the card."

They left the store and Jarrod stood by the window, watching them walk away. It had been a most unusual exchange. He'd lied because ... because ... he wasn't sure who they really were or what he should tell them. He prided himself on making decisions, being proactive. But this was a very different set of circumstances. A young man was dead—a man who had been in the store just three days ago. Mr. K was acting oddly and taking off more than usual. And now two strangers had come in asking questions he felt he could not answer, not without talking to Mr. K first.

He hurried to the phone behind the counter and dialed Deidrich Keller's home number. After four rings it went to an answering machine and Jarrod hung up. This was too important to leave a message and wait. He dialed again, this time Keller's cell phone. After two rings Deidrich answered. He would know it was Jarrod from the called ID.

"Yes, Jarrod?" he said.

Jarrod could not tell where his boss was, but he thought he heard traffic sounds in the background. Interesting; he had not gone home, or, if he had, he'd left again.

"Two people were just in the store," Jarrod said. "They claimed to have spoken to you earlier."

There was a moment of silence, then Deidrich Keller said, "Go on, Jarrod. What did they want to know?"

"They were asking about that young man who was murdered this week. I didn't tell them anything."

"Of course not, there's nothing to tell. Is there?"

Jarrod hesitated. He was questioning his own memory. Maybe he hadn't seen Mr. K talking to the young man, maybe it was a different young man entirely. "No, nothing to tell, Mr. K."

"What else did they want to know?"

"If you'd ever been away from the store for an extended period—you know, like your time in Berlin."

"And what did you tell them?"

Jarrod proceeded to inform Deidrich Keller of everything that had transpired with the couple—that the woman claimed to be a private detective, that they wanted his home address (which Jarrod did not give them), and that odd question about any extended absence.

D remained calm through it all. A sense of peaceful finality had come over him. He was glad Jarrod had not given them his home address. It was a home he would be leaving very soon, but he had one more task at hand, one more mission to accomplish. He told Jarrod he'd done well and that he would see him in the morning. It was a lie. He intended never to see Jarrod Sperling again.

32

A peace had come over Danny since he'd arrived at Margaret's Passion that morning. He knew it was part of an inevitable acceptance—accepting that Margaret Bowman was leaving, accepting that a large part of the world he had known and loved was changing. Margaret had lived a long and fruitful life. She'd achieved her dreams and touched so many people's lives. She had loved her husband, Gerard, with the same passion that gave her restaurant its name. Danny had never met Gerard Bowman, who died in a freak traffic accident just outside the restaurant two years before Danny was hired. He'd been a smoker, something Margaret disdained but indulged provided he went outside. So several times a day Gerard Bowman could be seen on the side street smoking a cigarette. One day he stepped off the curb to stamp out his cigarette butt in the gutter, and a taxi came flying through the light to make it across before it turned red. The driver saw Gerard in the street, was startled by the sight and swerved, losing control of the taxi. Ten seconds later Gerard Bowman was dead.

Margaret had carried on. She met Danny, hired him, and eleven years later she was leaving him. That was the part—the feeling—he had finally managed to make peace with. She was eighty-one years old. She was more than entitled to spend her last few years with her sister who was almost ninety. The restaurant was Danny's, and now

Margaret had completed the transfer of the only thing that had kept her here by deeding the building to him. She was passing it all on, saying, Here, it's yours now. I'm entrusting it to you. I know you'll make me proud.

Danny was thinking of that—making Margaret proud by surviving in the business, being a landlord soon, and giving the old woman the most amazing going away party New York City had ever seen—when a man walked into the restaurant. It was almost two o'clock. The kitchen stopped serving lunch at two, but Danny had never told a customer it was too late, not until the kitchen was actually closed. The man had fifteen more minutes, which meant he would be seated, he would be given a menu, and he would be served.

"Good afternoon," Danny said. Chloe was in the back room stocking shelves and Trebor was behind the bar. There were two women on stools finishing an early afternoon glass of wine. No one else was there.

"Good afternoon," D said. "I hope I'm not too late for a small bite. I've just come back from Berlin and I'm famished."

"No, no, not at all, please come in. Any table you'd like."

D chose a table well away from the window—unusual during the day, Danny thought, but some people didn't like the light. Danny walked with the man to a two-top near the bar and handed him a menu once he sat down.

"Your waiter will be with you in a moment. In the meantime, is there something you'd like from the bar?"

"Just water," D said. "Thank you."

D watched the man disappear around the corner of the bar. He didn't know if he'd bring the water himself or if a waiter would do that. He looked around the restaurant and was quite pleased with what he saw. He'd heard of Margaret's Passion, of course. One does not own a high-end clothing store with upper crust clients without hearing of the places they patronize. The Plaza. Elaine's, when there was an Elaine. The 21 Club. And Margaret's Passion. It was comfortable in a way newer eateries catering to the nouveau riche and the hangers-on were not. The trend these days, dismaying to people like Deidrich Keller, was for deafeningly loud restaurants where shouting was the only way to be heard by the person sitting across a small table from you. No, this was much more ... classy. More stylish, for those who knew what true style was.

He watched the man go into the kitchen, then return looking perplexed. He spoke briefly to the bartender, retrieved a glass of ice water and returned with it to the table.

"I'll be taking your order today," Danny said. He'd gone back to find Clarence, the waiter he expected to still be on duty, but was told by the cook that Clarence had taken off early, expecting no one else to come in. Chloe was still working on the dinner set up and Danny didn't want to bother her, so he decided to take the man's order himself. Danny set the water glass down. "Have you had a chance to decide?"

"Not quite yet," D said. "By the way, my name's Deidrich Keller. And you are?"

Danny was embarrassed. Introducing yourself was the first lesson of table service, but he had not taken anyone's order in a very long time.

"Danny Durban," he said. "My apology for neglecting to introduce myself."

"No apology needed. Are you the maître d?"

"No, no. I'm the owner."

"Ah," said D. "I feel special now." He glanced around. "I'd foolishly assumed someone named Margaret would be the owner of Margaret's Passion."

"She was, until very recently. Margaret Bowman."

"Is she deceased?"

"No. I ... my partner and I bought the restaurant from her. But she'll be moving away soon. The restaurant won't be the same without her. We'll survive, but there's only one Margaret Bowman."

D pretended that a thought had suddenly come to him. "You and your partner, you say?"

"Yes, his name's Kyle."

"What a small world! I met him just this morning. He said you were looking for a new suit."

Danny sighed. He remembered Kyle saying they were going to a men's store and assumed Kyle had taken it upon himself to suit shop for him. Kyle knew he was looking for something special for Margaret's party. "I am, yes," Danny said.

"Well then," said D, taking out a business card from his wallet. "I'm just the person for you. I'm a business owner myself. Keller and Whitman, clothing for the gentleman's gentleman."

The name rang a bell this time. Some of the customers at Margaret's got their clothes there—impeccably tailored suits, and shirts that cost enough as a dinner for four. It wasn't a place Danny would ever shop given the prices, and why he hadn't remembered it when Kyle said they were going there that morning.

"Here," D said, taking a pen from his jacket pocket and writing his cell number on the card. "I'll tell you what, call me anytime and we'll do a private fitting. I know this event is important to you—how could it not be?—and I'd like you to look your absolute best. I'll measure you myself and get you something done by the time of your party."

"It's a month from now," Danny said.

"Then we have plenty of time." D handed him the card. "Promise you'll call." Then, as if he'd just remembered something urgent, he said, "Oh, my ..."

"What?"

"I have to leave for London Friday. I won't be back until August. I'm looking at store locations there. But I don't do the stitching myself, of course!"

"Of course not," Danny said.

"I could size you and get an order in before I go. How about this afternoon?"

Danny hesitated. He'd never met this man before, but he knew the store's reputation. And it would be amazing to show up at Margaret's party in a suit from one of the city's best men's stores. "I'm not sure, I was planning ..."

"I'll give you a discount," D said, smiling. "A very deep discount."

How could Danny say no? It might even lift his spirits and put him in the frame of mind he wanted to be in: to view and experience Margaret's going away as a celebration, not a funeral procession or a wake.

Danny took the card. "It's a deal," he said. "Just let me get things wrapped up here and I'll call. Shall I meet you at the store?"

"Oh, no, Mr. Durban. This will be a private fitting. Just give me a call and I'll provide directions."

Danny put the card in his shirt pocket. "And now," he said, "order anything you'd like. Lunch is on the house."

"Very, very kind," D said, turning his attention to the menu. He was hungry now, and planned to eat a hearty meal before heading back to his townhouse to wait for a phone call. It was going to be an excellent evening, an intimate affair—his own going away party for two.

33

Few things unnerved Kyle more than speeding through Manhattan in a taxi. The drivers obeyed few rules, except the ones that could get them ticketed, and even those they skirted as often as they could. Lanes meant nothing to them, and they would veer wildly from side to side, maneuvering at high speeds through a sea of cars, trucks and buses. Double parking was common, especially during the week, and the flow of vehicles often made him think of clotted arteries, with cars as blood cells making their way around stops and knots.

This afternoon it was the opposite problem that had him fretting in the back seat with Linda: the President of the United States was in town, and traffic had come to a stop. They were idling at the corner of 49th Street and Lexington Avenue as traffic cops held everyone at a standstill, their arms out stiff and their whistles blowing.

"What the hell is *that?*" Linda asked, as they watched the longest motorcade either of them had ever seen turn onto Lexington Avenue and head south. The avenue had been closed to traffic, with police cars and motorcycle cops stationed at every street crossing.

"That," Kyle said, "is the Presidential motorcade." He knew this because his boss Imogene was scheduled to do a segment for Tokyo Pulse from a gala at the New York Public Library that night, with the President as the featured guest. Had he been working he might have been able to go as her assistant, but even the President of the United States couldn't keep him from taking time off to spend with Detective Linda. After all, there would always be another president.

They waited nervously in the back seat as the motorcade seemed to go on forever. Even the cab driver was impressed, gawking at block after block of black SUVs, many with SWAT types perched in the open backs, ready to jump out and fire in the event of an attack.

"What do we do now?" Linda asked, resigned to waiting for the motorcade to pass, the way one sits at a railroad crossing watching freight cars go by in a crawl.

"We re-group," Kyle said. "We go back to the apartment, we talk it through."

"When do we go to the police?"

"Today, I imagine. I just want to consider everything. I don't want to accuse a man wrongly, I don't want to assume that just because he spoke to Victor he killed him."

"But that's what you think."

"That's what I think, yes. If he didn't do it, if he's not the Pride Killer, then he's involved somehow."

"You mean he doesn't work alone?"

"It's not unheard of. And remember, if we move too quickly, we tip our hand. Who knows what might happen then. He might vanish again and we'd never catch him."

Kyle watched as the end of the motorcade finally passed by. They waited awhile longer as the traffic slowly started up again. Kyle felt his foot twitching furiously—they'd lost precious time waiting for the most powerful man in the world to pass by in one of those dozens of black SUVs (surely not the sedan with the Presidential flags flying from the hood, that had to be a decoy).

"It takes them awhile," the driver said, sensing his passengers' impatience. "They block all these streets, then they have to open them again, maybe five more minutes. You in a hurry?"

"Yes," they both said from the back seat.

"Let's just walk," Kyle said. "We can talk along the way. It's good for the thought processes."

"But it's twenty blocks."

"This is New York City. Twenty blocks is like walking across the street. Come on, we can bounce ideas off each other."

Kyle told the driver they were getting out. He handed a ten dollar bill through the plastic divider separating the front and back seats and opened the door. They could walk almost as quickly as the cab would get them there, especially if there were any more delays. And they could talk. They had the Pride Killer in their sights with one good shot at him and could not afford to miss.

34

Danny's usual routine was to go home for the break between lunch service and dinner. The bar at Margaret's Passion remained open starting at noon, but meals were only available for the two sittings. It had always been this way at the restaurant and always would be. Bar food was for bars, and Margaret's was definitely not in that class.

Once the kitchen closed each day, Danny would walk the fifteen minutes it took him to get home around two-thirty in the afternoon, then return at five to oversee the beginning of the dinner shift. He did not stay the entire evening—he never had, he was the day manager for all those years before he became the owner—but he liked being there for an hour or so ahead of time, especially now that Margaret's was his. His night manager, Patrice, did a terrific job and had been Danny's right hand for six years now. Combined with his recent promotion of Chloe to day manager, the pair gave Danny the level of comfort he needed with the business.

He couldn't hear Margaret upstairs; the staff had never been able to hear the Bowmans in the apartment above them. But he knew she was there, puttering around, most likely starting to slowly pack for the move to Florida. He thought about going up to see her for a few minutes, but he'd been upstairs once already today and didn't want to be a nuisance. Besides, he knew the impulse to spend time with her would only become more frequent as the time drew closer for her to leave. He thought about calling Kyle to let him know he was going for a private fitting but decided against it. The last text he'd had from Kyle was an hour ago, when they were canvassing an Upper East Side neighborhood to see if anyone recognized the photo they had of Victor Campagna. Poor Victor, Danny thought, as he stared another moment out the window onto 3rd Avenue. Poor Vinnie! The brothers were very close. The entire Campagna family must be in terrible distress. There'd been nothing more on the news about the two murders. Danny wondered if the Pride Killer—assuming that's who was behind this—would once again slip into the shadows.

"A penny for your thoughts," Chloe said, startling him.

Danny turned around to see her drying her hands on a towel. Chloe had not changed a bit since her promotion. She would still bus a table if needed, bartend or wash dishes. It was in her nature.

"A penny won't get you much anymore," Danny said.

"A dollar then."

"Just sad, that's all. But it'll be this way for the next month until she's gone." He nodded at the ceiling. "And for quite some time afterward, I imagine."

"Is there anything I can do? Short of talking her into staying."

"Nothing, but thank you." Danny took the business card out of his pocket. "Say, listen, I'm going out for a fitting ..." Chloe looked at him curiously. "For a suit."

"Ah."

"If Kyle calls, don't tell him. It want it to be a surprise. He went looking for a suit for me, you see, and I ... oh, never mind. Just tell him I'm running some errands. I'll be home by five. We're having dinner out tonight with our friend Linda."

"Will do."

Danny took the card in hand, pulled out his cell phone and dialed the private number Deidrich Keller had written on it. He figured two and a half hours was plenty of time to get to where Keller lived, be fitted for a fabulous new suit, and make it back to Gramercy Park by five.

Keller picked up on the second ring.

35

D had barely settled into his living room after a taxi ride home when his cell phone rang. He looked at the caller ID and saw Margaret's Passion listed. He let it ring twice before answering, staring at the phone as his smile grew wider. He'd been successful in enticing Danny Durban with his gracious offer of a private fitting. He'd been imagining it all the way back in the cab and here it was, about to become a reality.

"Deidrich Keller," he said, putting the phone on speaker so he could hold it in his lap.

"Yes, Mr. Keller, this is Danny Durban, from the restaurant."

"Mr. Durban! Let me guess, you'd like that fitting after all. And that deep discount! I'm so glad you took me up on my offer. Unless of course I'm mistaken and there's some other reason you're calling."

"No, you're absolutely correct. I've just finished up for the afternoon here and I was wondering if this would be a good time to stop by."

"Let me check my calendar," D said. He counted to five, then said, "Fortunately, I have nothing going until this evening. How soon could you be here?"

"As soon as a taxi can get there. By the way, I'll need to know where 'there' is."

D thought about it moment. Should he stick to protocol and give this man a false address several blocks away, then feign stupidity and walk him back? Or did it not matter, considering he would be on a plane by midnight? Danny, unlike like all the others, would not be in the East River but left in the basement as a grand farewell—he'd decided to let them find out who he was, who he *had been*. This was his pièce de résistance, his big going-away, after which he would be leaving for Europe. First stop: Berlin. He'd already checked into flights and booked one late that night. Yes, he hated Berlin. He hated the country, the people and the language, but he was no fool. He'd survived as the Pride Killer for seven years—albeit three in absentia—and he would reemerge again, somewhere, when the time was ready. But this was his last hurrah in a city he'd grown tired of, his curtain call as Deidrich Keller, owner of Keller and Whitman, master of etiquette and the slow kill.

"Do you have a pen handy?" D said. Danny said yes, and D gave him the address of the townhouse. Not two blocks away, not transposed or inverted. The real address of the real home where the very, very real Deidrich Keller lived and so many others had died. He intended for Danny to join them soon, after which Deidrich Keller would vanish, leaving behind him nothing but a ghastly mystery.

36

Kyle and Linda walked into the apartment exactly twenty minutes after leaving the taxi. They'd talked everything over on the walk and both were convinced the key to finding the killer was Deidrich Keller. Neither was certain yet it was Keller himself—he didn't seem the type to be killing men and dumping their bodies in the East River. But, Kyle wondered, is there such a thing as a serial killer type? Most of the good ones—*successful* ones, he corrected himself, as he closed the door and set his keys on the small table in their entryway—did not look like serial killers. They looked like neighbors, co-workers, even fathers and favored sons. Once in a while they were daughters!

Smelly and Leonard had heard them coming down the hallway and were waiting at the door. They never ran out into the hallway, seeming to think it led somewhere dreadful and scary for curious cats, but they would perch close enough to make opening the door a challenge.

"That's odd," said Kyle, shooing them away with his foot. "Danny always gives them treats when he gets home in the afternoon." Then, to the cats, "What's up, kids? Didn't Danny give you snacks?"

"I don't think he's here," Linda said.

She was right. The apartment was completely quiet. Normally, Danny also turned on the television in the bedroom to get caught up on the news with one of the cable channels. Today there was silence.

"He must've run errands. Or maybe he's visiting with Margaret," Kyle said. "I know he's been spending more time with her before she leaves."

He gave Danny's absence no more thought as they settled back into the apartment. Linda took off her jacket, exposing her gun in its shoulder holster, and sat on one of the two small couches they had in the living room. This one faced the window, and she could see a nearly identical apartment building facing them from across Lexington Avenue. New York City struck her as the perfect place to have a pair of binoculars, if you were given to seeing what your neighbors were up to without them knowing.

"Do you ever think about being watched?" she asked, peering out the window.

"Excuse me?" Kyle said. He'd gone into the kitchen to make them coffee. He'd also grabbed the small box of cat treats from a shelf and placed a half dozen of them on the floor, where Smelly and Leonard quickly gobbled them up. He could see Linda from where he knelt just inside the kitchen door.

"I mean, you can see into other people's apartments here. And they can see you. Does that ever bother you?"

"That's what drapes are for," he called back, standing and returning to the coffee. "Besides, you get used to it. After a while you don't think about it anymore. Are they watching? Are they not watching? Some people want them to, you know."

"The exhibitionists."

"Yes, and there's no shortage of those in New York City. It's see-and-be-seen for too many people living here. Danny and I don't give it any thought. Unless I'm naked after a shower and I suddenly realize it, and it's like, ooops, I'd better put a towel around me. Otherwise having people see into your windows is like background noise, you can't even hear it after a few weeks." Watching coffee drip into a cup, he said, "Let me see if I remember ... creamer, no sugar."

"Perfect."

Kyle finished making their coffee and brought the two cups into the living room. He set them on the coffee table in front of Linda and took a seat on the matching couch across from her.

"Let me just check," he said, taking his cell phone off his belt clip. He looked at the message icon. "Nope, no text. No email. I'm guessing he went to the grocery store. We ran out of milk this morning." He hooked his phone back onto his belt, then took a sip of his coffee. "So what do we know?"

"We know the Pride Killer has struck twice in forty-eight hours. That's the first and most important thing we need to keep in mind."

"Right. A third is coming very soon unless we get past speculation into action."

"But action and accusation are two different things," Linda said. "What else do we know?"

"We know Victor Campagna went to Cargill's for a drink with his friend Sam Paddington, but Sam never showed up. He then left Cargill's and made his way to Keller and Whitman to look for a suit."

"Deidrich Keller said he was alone there that day—something I don't think we can take as gospel truth—and never saw Victor."

"But the bodega owner *did* see him," said Kyle. "And he saw him come out of Keller and Whitman's.

"Maybe Jarrod was working by himself that morning, we haven't considered that."

"So why would Keller say he was there alone?"

"To cover for Jarrod. We don't know what their relationship is outside work."

"Jarrod as the Pride Killer? The man seems like too much dust would unnerve him."

"Could be a front. Never assume there's a type in these cases. It's also possible the bodega owner was mistaken. Or lying."

"He'd have no reason to lie," said Kyle.

"For his moment of fame? Maybe he wants to be on the news. But I doubt it. I think he was telling the truth. I think the one lying here is Deidrich Keller. But is he lying to protect himself, or someone else?"

"Maybe he doesn't want to get involved. Saying he saw a dead man just before the dead man's trail grows cold could bring a lot of suspicion."

"So," said Linda, sipping her coffee and setting it back on a coaster. "Do we confront Deidrich Keller, or do we go to the police with what we think?"

Kyle considered it for several seconds, then said, "I think we have one last conversation with Keller, but we take him by surprise."

"How's that?"

"We go to his home. He won't be expecting us, and it will throw him off his game, if he's playing one."

"And it will get us inside that house ... or apartment, whichever it is. I'd like to see it for myself, get a sense of the place."

"Any secrets it might be hiding."

Linda instinctively touched her gun. Secrets could sometimes be fatal.

"There's only one problem," Kyle said. "We don't know where he lives. I tried finding an address with my cell phone but there's nothing listed. There's really nothing about Deidrich Keller at all online, except the store. That's quite an accomplishment in the digital age."

"Let me make a call," Linda said. She reached down and took her cell phone from her purse on the floor.

"You're calling Information? Does that even exist anymore?"

"Not the kind of information you're thinking of," she said. "Remember, I'm a retired cop, with friends on the force."

"In New Hope, Pennsylvania. This is Manhattan."

"It doesn't matter. When it comes to digging up information, nothing gets it done like a call from a police department."

"I hope you're right ..."

Linda held her finger up to her lips, silencing Kyle. "Hey, Marty, what's up?" she said into her phone. "It's Linda Sikorsky. Listen, I'm trying to get an address on someone who doesn't want to be found. Can you help me out?"

She listened carefully as her ex-colleague on the other end of the line went about trying to help her.

Kyle finished the last of his coffee and took their cups back into the kitchen, followed closely by the cats. It was they, and not the person giving them treats, who decided how many were enough. Kyle fished several more out of the pouch and put them on the floor.

After several minutes, Linda thanked Marty and walked quickly into the kitchen. "Got it," she said. "He's on East 82nd Street. No apartment number."

"Probably a townhouse," Kyle said. "The Upper East Side is full of them."

"So let's go. He'll never expect to see us on his doorstep."

Kyle rinsed out the coffee cups and left them in the sink. He led Linda to the door, grabbing his keys from the stand. "I have to let Danny know where we are," he said as they hurried into the hallway.

"Call him from the taxi. We're definitely not walking this time."

Kyle felt a slight annoyance with Danny for not sending a message. On the other hand, Danny knew Kyle was with Linda and probably thought they were still out somewhere on the trail. Danny wisely kept his distance from the chaos Kyle and Linda always found themselves in. He thought it was dangerous and preferred not knowing to worrying constantly. Kyle would call him once they were on their way. The very least he owed Danny was letting him know they were okay.

37

"This is quite a nice home you have," Danny said. He'd arrived at Deidrich Keller's townhouse ten minutes earlier after a surprisingly quick cab ride from the restaurant. Synchronized green lights had gotten them twenty blocks without a stop; the rest was unusually light traffic for a Thursday afternoon.

"Thank you, Mr. Durban," D said. He was standing to the side, watching as Danny took in the living room with its fireplace and paintings.

"Please, call me Danny."

"Danny, then."

"Is that your grandfather?" Danny was looking at the same painting Scott Devlin admired the day before. D had bought the painting at a flea market for $50.

"My great uncle, actually. When the family still had its fortune, before ... well, everything comes and goes."

"I'm sorry," said Danny, not sure why he would be. Judging from the townhouse, Deidrich Keller was not poor and probably never had been. But Danny knew from working with wealthy customers that for many of them, being down to their last million dollars meant destitution was not far off.

"May I offer you a drink?" D said, still watching Danny from behind. He decided he'd made a good choice, both in terms of his victim and in his plan. He would have an afternoon to remember—and to be remembered by—then he would cease to exist for all intents and purposes. The memories would be his forever, and he would start anew, as another man, another killer. The anticipation was nearly too much for him to contain.

"I don't normally drink in the afternoon," Danny said. He turned from the painting.

"Please, have a seat." D motioned to the plush couch. Danny walked the few steps over and sat down.

"Very comfortable."

"I hope so. And even more comfortable with a glass of Chardonnay."

"I really shouldn't."

"It can't possibly hurt. We'll visit a while, enjoy some wine, then I'll take your measurements and show you my private catalog. You'll be on your way in less than an hour and the finest suit you've ever owned will be yours in a week. I promise."

Danny thought a moment more about it, then said yes, a glass of wine would be nice. The last few days had been especially stressful, with the party planning, the emotions of Margaret's leaving, and now having Detective Linda visiting for Pride weekend. Danny and Kyle weren't much into the annual festivities and had not been to a parade in years, but Kyle wanted Linda to have a good time, something to remember before going to tend to her dying mother-in-law. Danny would not let the strain of it all show—at least not to Linda.

D went to the liquor cabinet. A small refrigerator was tucked in beneath it. He reached inside and took out an unopened bottle of the best Chardonnay he'd been able to find. Two minutes later he'd poured them each a glass, with something special in Danny's. He took the glasses back to the living room and found Danny still seated on the couch, admiring the chandelier hanging over him.

"This really is quite a home," Danny said, taking the glass from D.

"Can you believe I got it for a steal? When I bought here, prices were still low and the Upper East Side was not the place to be. They practically begged me to buy this house. So I did. I made it my own, fixed everything up, and now it's worth three times what I paid for it. Are you looking to buy?"

"No," Danny said, laughing. "Kyle and I are apartment people, at least as long as we live in New York. Someday we may head out to suburbia, or maybe the New Jersey countryside—we love it there—but not townhouses in Manhattan, thanks anyway."

Danny began to feel just a bit dizzy. "I knew I shouldn't have had a drink this early."

"It's nothing. Just the first flush of a good wine." D took a sip from his own glass. "Speaking of which, I have some remarkable wines in the cellar. I know Margaret's Passion only serves the best of the best. Might you be interested?"

Danny was definitely feeling the wine now. "I'm always looking for the finest for my customers. Cuts of meat, staff, tea, and certainly wine. We have a sommelier, I should probably have her take a look at your collection."

"Excellent idea, we can set something up as soon as I return from London. In the meantime, come, have a look yourself. It's quite an extensive wine cellar, one of the best in the city, I've been told."

Danny wasn't a wine connoisseur but he'd always been fascinated by the subculture of those who were. The temperature controlled rooms, the obscene prices paid for a single bottle of fermented grape juice. One of his favorite shows on the Food Channel featured an obnoxious host named Claire Cracken who went around the world telling people their $2,500 bottle of 1865 Chateau-Something was worthless and tasted like vinegar. He couldn't pass up the chance to see what Deidrich had in his basement.

"Sure," Danny said. "Then the fitting! I haven't mentioned to Kyle that I was coming here, it's a surprise. It was sweet of him to go suit shopping for me, but I'm very particular. Don't tell him I said that."

"I won't say a word."

Could the situation be more perfect? He now knew what no one else did: Danny Durban had come to his home without telling anyone where he was going. Perhaps the stars were shining on him, right here, in broad daylight in Manhattan, to make up for the near-fatal mistake he'd made with Victor Someone. He was being repaid, he thought, and quite handsomely.

"Let's take a quick look at the wine cellar, perhaps select something you can take to your sommelier as an example, then we'll come back up for the fitting and you'll be on your way."

"Excellent," Danny said, as D led the way to the basement door. Danny had gone from feeling lightheaded to giddy as well, and decided there would not be a second glass of wine.

D opened the basement door and flipped on the light. A set of carpeted stairs lead down. The entire basement was carpeted for soundproofing, except for his special room, his *real* fitting room. He'd wanted the floor in there to be easy to clean. He felt the thrill course through him as the killing time ticked closer by the second.

"Please," D said, holding the door for Danny. "You first."

Danny handed his glass of wine to D, saying, "Hold this please, I feel a little woozy," and started down the stairs.

D looked at the glass, seeing it was nearly empty. He smiled as broad a smile as had graced his face in months. He waited until Danny was nearly at the bottom of the stairs, then he closed the door and followed.

38

"That's odd," Kyle said, as the taxi rolled through 34th Street heading north. "Danny's not answering his phone."

Kyle had sent a text message as soon as they'd hopped in the cab in front of the apartment building. Danny was always very good at responding. Kyle texted again, "Where are you?" and heard nothing back. Finally, he did something he rarely did since the normalization of texting and emails: he dialed Danny's phone number. After four rings it went to voicemail.

"Maybe he's indisposed," Linda said, meaning perhaps Danny was in a men's room somewhere.

"No, he always responds. This is weird. I'm going to call the restaurant."

Linda watched out the window as they passed 38th Street, then 42nd, counting as the numbers slowly went up. She calculated they would be at Keller's townhouse within ten minutes, probably sooner.

"Chloe?" Danny said into his cell phone. "Is Danny still there? I can't get him to reply to my texts or calls."

Chloe proceeded to tell him that Danny had left an hour ago. As she'd been promised to secrecy by Danny she did not say where he went, only that he had some errands to run and he'd be home by five.

"Listen, Chloe," Danny said, "if he comes back or he calls, tell him to call me ASAP. It's very important."

The urgency in Kyle's voice made Chloe hesitate. "Is anything wrong? Are the cats okay?"

"Smelly and Leonard are fine, but I need to find Danny. If he comes back in or calls ask him to reach me immediately."

"Kyle, listen," Chloe said. "You didn't hear this from me, but Danny went out for a suit."

Linda saw Kyle's expression change.

"A suit?"

"Yeah," Chloe replied, her voice tinny through the phone.

"Hang on, Chloe, I'm putting you on speaker." A second later they could hear her voice filling the back seat as Kyle said, "You still there?"

"I'm still here."

"So what's this about a suit?"

"Well, there was this guy who came in late for lunch, just about time to close the kitchen. You know Danny, he never turns anyone away unless he has to. So he served him."

"What did this man look like, Chloe?"

"Tallish. Handsome. Older for sure, in his forties. Said he'd just got back from Europe and he owned a suit store, men's store, whatever."

Linda mouthed the words, "Oh my God" and started to say something, but Kyle shushed her.

"So what happened then?" he asked

"Then? The guy left. He ate, gave Danny his card, and left."

"Chloe, thank you for the information. It's very, very helpful."

Kyle was about to hang up when Chloe said, "Kyle? Please don't tell Danny I told you. He wanted me to keep it a secret. About the suit, I mean."

Kyle laughed for the first time in two days. "Well, I knew you didn't mean about the man, Chloe. Danny's not the straying sort.

His eye might wander, all eyes do, but that's as far afield as we go. And don't worry, if this is the man I think it was, Danny will be very relieved you told me."

Kyle hung up. The taxi was now at 72nd Street and they had a decision to make.

"Do we go to the store instead?" Kyle said. "Danny left an hour ago, he's probably there now."

Linda was undecided: should they veer from their plans and head to the store, or stay on mission. The store wasn't that far from the townhouse, they could do both, but first she wanted to make sure Keller wasn't home.

"Let's stay on track," she said. "We'll go to the townhouse, have the taxi wait outside while we see if Keller's home, then make a beeline to the store. If Keller's the Pride Killer, he's not claiming his victims at a highly visible store on Lexington Avenue. If Danny's there, he's safe for the moment."

Kyle sighed—a deep exhale of anxiety and adrenaline. He was perched on the very edge of the backseat now. They were just a block away from the townhouse. He leaned up to the partition, handed the driver a $20 and said, "Listen, we need you to wait when we get there. Keep the meter running. If no one's home we have a second stop. If this person *is* home, just keep the change and go."

"Fine," said the driver. It was the only word he'd uttered in fifty blocks.

39

Danny listened in horror as his cell phone buzzed. He kept it on vibrate at the restaurant, and now, helpless, he heard it shaking and rattling just out of reach. He knew it must be Kyle—Chloe and the others at Margaret's only called him in cases of emergency, knowing he needed his away-time from the demands of the job.

He had no idea how long he'd been unconscious. Obviously long enough for Deidrich Keller to get him to a gurney and secure him with straps. He was still fully clothed, which was a very minor relief. He also knew he had fallen into the trap of the man known for years as the elusive Pride Killer. How could he be so stupid, he wondered. How could he not have realized that while there were coincidences in life all the time, having Deidrich Keller come into the restaurant for lunch just hours after Kyle and Linda spoke to him was not one of them? Had his judgment been dulled by all the emotions of the past few months? Had he let his guard down so far he had no instincts left—if he'd ever had them at all? How, exactly, did he allow himself to be lured into this position, which may well prove to be his last?

"It's your husband," D said, glancing at the phone and seeing Kyle's name on the caller ID. "Shall I answer it?"

Danny knew the man was toying with him. He wouldn't be surprised if he answered the phone to torture Kyle with the knowledge of what was about to happen. Danny said nothing, hoping his silence would keep Keller from taking the call.

"No," said D, letting the phone ring a fourth time and go into voicemail. "Better he and that bitch he's with find out about you when it's too late."

"What are you going to do?" Danny said, his voice hoarse as his wits slowly came back to him.

"Do you know who I am?"

"You're the Pride Killer."

"Then that answers your question."

Danny felt himself growing damp with sweat, yet the basement was nearly cold from an air conditioner he could see mounted in a small blacked-out window in a far corner of the ceiling. He forced himself to become fully alert, lifting his head as far as he could—there was a restraint of some kind lashed across his forehead. A belt? A strap? He couldn't tell, but he was able to bend his head up just a bit, and turn his neck slightly from side to side.

He was not in the main basement room, he was sure of that. He'd made it to the bottom of the stairs ... it was coming back to him now. He'd felt his knees begin to wobble as he got down the stairs and into the well-furnished cellar. Deidrich Keller had taken pains to make his killer's lair as deceptively arranged as his townhouse. There was a large leather couch and two matching armchairs, Danny remembered that. There was some kind of artwork on the walls, imitation modern art that reminded Danny of Pollock and Warhol, one above the couch, another above a low ebony cabinet. There was indeed a wine cellar of sorts, with rows and rows of dark bottles carefully stacked in a waist-high rack that ran along the back wall. Danny had been about to comment on the comfort of the room when he realized the wooziness he'd been feeling was not natural. His legs began to buckle and he lunged for the couch, saying, "What did you do to me?" as he fell face-first onto the cushions.

"What I did to you," Danny remembered Keller saying just before he lost consciousness, "is nothing compared to what I'm going to do."

Then all was blackness, and now this. In a separate room. Cold but sweating with fear. Knowing Kyle had been trying to call, knowing rescue was just beyond his arm's reach. Watching as a sadistic, very successful serial killer hummed to himself and stood in front of a tray, his back to Danny, inspecting tools that Danny could see just on the periphery of his vision. Torture tools. The kind of instruments from hell the living only see as they are about to die.

The taxi pulled up in front of Deidrich Keller's townhouse. Linda was out immediately, hurrying up the steps with Kyle a moment behind. The cab idled at the curb as promised.

Kyle caught up to Linda at the top step as Linda pushed the door buzzer and waited. After a long minute without response, she pushed the buzzer again.

"He's not here," Kyle said, taking Linda by the arm. "Let's go to the store."

"Wait just a minute, I'm not so sure …" She cocked her head and listened.

"What are you …"

"Shh!" She listened carefully, as if she heard a very small voice on the wind. She slowly turned her head, looking for the source of the sound. Kyle followed her line of sight, first up, then to the side, and finally down. There were basement window wells, and in one of them a small air conditioner could be heard humming.

"There," Linda said. "An air conditioner."

"In the basement. Why would he have an air conditioner in the basement?"

"And why would it be on if he wasn't home?" She pushed the door buzzer again, this time hard enough that Kyle thought she might push it through the wall.

D heard the buzzer upstairs. So did Danny, though he tried to keep any trace of hope or excitement off his face.

"I'm very well equipped down here," D said, turning back from his tray. He held what looked like an X-Acto knife in his hand. "You know, I've always been quick about it, preferring a belt or garrote of some kind—not for mercy, but for the mess. I mean, really, who needs the clean up? But I've gone to some trouble for you, acquiring a few extra toys just this morning." He held up the knife. "Art supplies, indeed." He then nodded to another corner of the room, behind Danny. "You can't see it from where you are, but there's a small monitor mounted in the corner. I can see whoever's at the front door. Would you like to know who it is?"

Danny swallowed hard, afraid of the answer. Was it the police? Would this madman simply ignore them and hope they went away? *Please, please don't go away*, Danny prayed, licking his drying lips.

"It's your husband and the bitch. She's looking around. My mistake! She probably heard the air conditioner."

Danny discovered in that instant that hope and despair can be felt at the same time. He hoped Kyle and Linda would not go away, that they would know something was happening in this house of horrors. Yet he despaired they would leave and he would never see his husband, his friends, his cats, anything that mattered to him, ever again.

D put the knife back on the tray. "I'd better go see what they want before they call in reinforcements," he said. "Don't worry, Danny. I'll be back." He took a roll of duct tape from the tray and hurried over to Danny. Peeling off a piece and cutting it with the knife, he taped Danny's mouth. "Can't have you shouting out now, can we?" he said.

Taking a deep breath, D composed himself. Danny watched in fascinated terror as Deidrich Keller's face changed, softening, smiling, becoming the face of an innocent man caught up in something he had nothing to do with. "This won't take long."

D left the room, humming to himself. Danny could hear the hum fade as the man who was very close to taking his life climbed the basement stairs and quietly closed the door behind him.

"He's here," Linda said. "I know he is." She rang the bell one more time. If Keller did not answer the door she was prepared to find a way in. Then, to their surprise, the door opened. Deidrich Keller stood in the doorway, feigning sleep, as if he'd been woken from a nap.

"Yes, Mr. Callahan, and Brenda, was it?"

"Linda Sikorsky."

"Right. I'd say it was nice to see you again but I've just been sleeping! I nap sometimes in the afternoon."

"May we come in?" Kyle asked. "We'd like to ask a few more questions."

"Certainly," said D, as he stepped aside, waving them into his home.

The three of them entered the foyer, tastefully furnished with an ebony crescent table and mirror just inside the door. Soft classical piano music played in the living room. Kyle identified it as Chopin, among his late father's favorites. "Let's head into the living room and sit," D said, leading them down the short hallway into his expansive living room.

Kyle looked around, taking in each detail. The paintings, the fireplace, the soft suede furniture. There were a number of photographs lined up on the fireplace mantel. Kyle wandered over and looked at them. He had the strange sensation no one in the pictures was related to Deidrich Keller. "Family?" he asked.

"Distant," said D. "Won't you have a seat?"

Linda eased down onto the couch. D could see she was still wearing the gun holster. His smile fell an inch or two. He remained standing as Kyle took a seat in the matching chair, forming a small triangle with Linda on one side, Kyle on the other, and Deidrich Keller standing by the coffee table.

"Now," D said. "May I get you something to drink?"

Danny could hear movement upstairs. The floorboards in the townhouse were old and original, and they'd warped over the years as old wood does. The constant shifting of cold to hot, damp to dry with the changing seasons, created curves in the boards. No matter how well they were kept up, they always creaked. He heard voices, too, but muffled. He recognized the timbre of Kyle's voice, speaking in short sentences. It elevated his agitation to a nearly unbearable level. Would Keller kill them, too? Would they all be found dead in this basement days from now, or be buried under the floor?

He tried to free his hands. His arms had been fastened with straps to the metal bars along the side of the gurney. His legs were bound with a belt and strapped down. There appeared to be no way to free himself, but he kept trying, wriggling his right hand back and forth. He told himself over and over to relax, just relax. He'd always been fascinated by escape artists, and he knew the key to extricating oneself from restraints was not to fight against them, but to surrender to them. Deep breaths. Let the body become fluid. Finally, after a full five minutes of letting himself become smaller and smaller, his right hand came free. At first he didn't realize it, but he felt the space that had opened up around his wrist, just enough empty space to allow him to slide his arm up and out. He raised his hand and stared at it, as if he couldn't believe what he was seeing. Then he quickly grabbed the tape on his mouth, yanked it off and screamed.

Kyle and Linda both declined D's offer of a drink. They did not want to waste time while he made coffee or tea, and they certainly were not having alcohol in the middle of the afternoon. When he'd made the offer, Linda glanced at Kyle with the very slightest shake of her head: no. Kyle read into it everything Linda wanted him to. Keller was stalling. Keller was up to something. Whatever he offered someone to drink in this house, it was a drink they regretted.

"We visited your store again," Kyle said.

"Yes, I know," D said. "Jarrod called me. He was afraid I might be in some danger."

"Danger?" said Linda.

"With this Pride Killer person on the loose, and apparently some connection to my store I'm completely unaware of. I realized after speaking with Jarrod that I had seen that young man, looking in the store window. He never came in, though. Do you suppose this killer is stalking his victims? Perhaps he followed the man, approached him outside my business, and that's where the trail went cold, so to speak."

"I think you know more than you're telling us," Kyle said. "I think it's time for us to go to the police and suggest they have a conversation with you."

D stared at them. "I have to ask you to leave now." His voice was cold, his smile gone and replaced by a flat, hard expression.

That was when they heard it: a loud scream from beneath them. A man shouting, "Help me! Help me!" And that man, Kyle instantly recognized, was Danny.

"Oh my God, he's here!" Kyle shouted. He jumped up from the couch. "Where is he?"

Without waiting for Keller to respond, Kyle hurried through the house, looking for doors, calling out, "We're here, Danny! We're here!"

Keller was alone in the living room now with Linda. Just as she rose from the couch he lunged at her, shoving her back into the cushions. She was a tall woman, but Deidrich Keller was taller, and stronger. He shoved his forearm against her throat. When she reached up with both hands to free herself, gasping, he grabbed her gun from its holster. Stepping back from the couch, he pointed the pistol directly at Linda's chest and said, "Stop right there."

Danny had not been successful in freeing his other arm. He'd also stopped relaxing, fighting frantically against his restraints. He heard the door open and footsteps rushing down the stairs. He looked up, shocked and relieved, to see Kyle running into the room.

Kyle hurried over to him. He didn't know what was going on upstairs, but he knew they had little time. He had to free Danny from the gurney. He stood over Danny, trying to determine where the buckles were on the straps.

"The knife," Danny said, nodding at the tray where Keller had his instruments of pain and pleasure. "Use the knife."

Kyle grabbed the X-Acto knife, turned back to the gurney and began slicing the straps. The knife wasn't meant to cut leather, but Kyle was determined. He cut himself slashing at the straps and a gush of blood began flowing from his fingers. He didn't care. He kept cutting, furiously digging with the knife blade. Finally the strap gave way and Danny was free. He slid off the gurney. He wanted to embrace Kyle, to fall into him, but there was no time. They were both about to run back upstairs when they heard the voice behind them.

"Let's all just stay in the basement, shall we?" D said.

Kyle turned around and saw Linda in front of Deidrich Keller, who was holding her gun, calmly and evenly, prepared to shoot her in the back.

"It will be so much easier to clean things up down here."

Kyle and Danny watched in horror as Keller raised the gun back over his shoulder. In a quick, savage arc, he brought the gun butt smashing against Linda Sikorsky's skull. She collapsed in an instant, as if she'd been inflated and all the air inside her suddenly released.

Kyle ran to her, fearful of the worst.

"I doubt she's dead," D said. "Probably just unconscious. She's in for quite a surprise when she wakes up again."

Timing was everything, Kyle knew. Decisions had to be made so quickly sometimes they could not be called decisions, but reactions, instincts. He was in a crouch over Linda. He still had the knife in his hand, and without thinking, without knowing what would happened next, he threw himself at Keller and thrust the knife into his leg.

Keller screamed. Kyle pulled the knife out and plunged it in again, causing Keller to collapse on the floor beside Linda.

Kyle scrambled for the gun. They two men struggled—Deidrich Keller was not giving up without a fight. Danny watched, terrified, as his husband and the man who had been close to killing them all rolled and wrestled on the floor. What could he do? Should he jump in and try to subdue Keller? Then he saw it: Keller had gotten the knife and was raising it over Kyle's back. He was going to bury it in Kyle's neck! Danny screamed, "Nooooo!"

Then a gunshot. One single, roaring gunshot. Danny feared the worst. It had come to this. Kyle and Linda's obsession with criminals, their repeated forays into the worlds of the depraved. His very worst nightmare had just become reality. He had to do something. He had to survive and do what he could to help them all. He turned to the instrument tray and grabbed a small, stainless steel hammer. With enough force it could be lethal. He turned back and the sight stunned him. Kyle standing up. Kyle rising slowly. First to his knees, then to his feet. Linda Sikorsky's gun was in his hand. Deidrich Keller was dead.

Kyle had never fired a gun in his life. He'd never held a gun. And yet, here he was in the basement of a townhouse owned by one of the most vicious and elusive serial killers New York City had ever seen. That killer was dead, and Kyle had killed him.

Linda stirred, moaning on the floor.

"She's alive," Danny said.

"He's not," said Kyle, looking into the open, lifeless eyes of Deidrich Keller. And then he said, simply, "Call the police."

40

Kyle wished it had been a dream. He lay in bed, staring up at the ceiling, afraid to look at the digital clock by the television. A muted sitcom re-run played on one of a hundred channels, the light from the screen flickering into the room. Danny was asleep beside him. Or at least he was pretending to be. Kyle stayed silent, not wanting to know if Danny, too, was wide awake on his side, reliving the last moments of the night before.

Kyle was consumed with guilt. Not for killing Deidrich Keller—lives had been saved by that gunshot, immeasurable pain had been spared his victims and his victims' families. But guilt for chasing killers in the first place. It had become a pastime for him, a way of amusing himself. Bo Sweetzer at Pride Lodge, Kieran Stipling from the Katherine Pride Gallery, Charlotte Gaines at CrossCreek Farm, and now the deadliest of them all, Deidrich Kristof Keller III. Dead by Kyle's own hand in an air-conditioned basement.

He'd thought the interrogations would never end. He, Linda and Danny spent most of the night at the police station giving statements, reliving what had happened, and answering over and over why they had not gone to the police with their suspicions. What was he supposed to tell them? *That it was too much fun chasing killers on their own?* That was the real answer, the answer that shocked him, like realizing something about ourselves we would never tell anyone and had not wanted to know.

It had to stop. Now was as good a time as any, too. So many things were about to change. So many shifts and rearrangements in life. Now was his chance to turn away from the dark side, to just be a personal assistant, amateur photographer, friend and husband. To live a normal life. Could he do it? Would he do it?

The answer is what had him awake at 3:00 a.m., blinking in the darkness.

The answer was no.

EPILOGUE

July came and went without the kind of heat Kyle was accustomed to in New York's summer months. On the whole it was shaping up to be one of the coolest summers they'd had in a decade. He was fine with that; the heat, stench and humidity of Manhattan between June and September were usually overwhelming. But not this year. This year had been different in so many ways.

He had killed a man. He'd pursued murderers before, but never had it come to this: struggling with someone who was determined to end his life in a feverish bid to save his own, wresting Linda's gun away, and then … without thinking about it, without even intending it, shooting Deidrich Keller in the heart. He didn't know he'd shot him in the heart until later, when an autopsy was performed. But he knew immediately Keller was dead, and he knew he had killed him when he lifted himself up from the floor, with Danny behind him and Linda just beginning to regain consciousness. It was a scene he would relive in his mind for years to come, perhaps for all the years he had left on the planet.

It was now August. The Pride parade had snaked down Fifth Avenue over a month ago and displayed its explosion of color without them. Linda would simply have to visit again, or find another parade to go to, although Kyle suspected she never would. For her, too, the memory of what happened had quickly become a stain. There was no way any of them was going to a parade after the events of that Thursday in the basement of an Upper East Side townhouse. By Friday morning everyone knew the Pride Killer was dead. The police knew. The media knew—including Kyle's boss Imogene, who for once in her life had the good sense not to press him for an exclusive interview. At least not until the following week. He turned her down.

The three of them gave exhaustive statements. The detectives they met took a very dim view of them pursuing a serial killer on their own. There was also the issue of Linda's firearm. New York City was famous for its gun laws and the whole thing had left them in a gray area. Kyle was the one doing the shooting. Kyle was not licensed to have, hold, shoot, or own a gun. But Kyle had somehow gotten the gun from Keller and ended the career of a killer who had confounded the NYPD for seven years. At the mayor's prodding, any idea of charges concerning the weapon were dropped. Kyle was hailed as a hero, a position he never sought or wanted to hold. It had made for a stressful, dreadful weekend, with the time they had to spend with Linda its only saving grace.

Linda Sikorsky had no problem with a dead serial killer. She also did not envy Kyle's sudden fame as the man who stopped the Pride Killer—a claim he would never make anyway. She had encountered many terrible things in her years as a cop and was able to put most of her feelings aside, down where she kept the fear she'd known on the job, the doubt, and the sorrow of having told so many people their loved ones were dead. She also had bigger concerns. Her wife was waiting for her in Phoenix with her dying mother-in-law. Life did not stop because a madman died quickly and deservedly in a New York City basement.

The three of them spent the rest of that weekend going around the city. They shopped, they sight-saw, they even went to a Broadway show for Saturday matinee. None of it made them forget what had happened, but it helped. Nothing could be changed, but Linda's time with them was limited and they spent it having as much enjoyment as they could. Then, early Monday, they said goodbye on the curb outside their apartment building as Linda got into a taxi and headed to the airport. Nothing would ever be quite the same.

In the six weeks since, parts of their world had shifted dramatically. Margaret Bowman had her going-away party, and it was a huge success. Also a very tearful one, as guest after guest toasted the old woman and offered anecdotes about what Margaret's Passion meant to them—a first date, a wedding anniversary, the signing of a contract to star in a movie. Danny did not buy a new suit after all and doubted he would be suit-shopping anytime soon. He gave the last toast of the night.

Two weeks later they got a call from Linda. She was still in Phoenix with Kirsten, making funeral arrangements. Dot McClellan had died the night before, quietly, as is usually the case with someone riddled with cancer and pumped full of opiates. All in all it had been a cool but very hard summer.

Now Linda and Kirsten were back in their small house in rural New Jersey. Linda was back at her vintage-everything store. Kirsten was taking pottery classes and wondering what she wanted to do now that she'd sold her real estate business. One thing she knew: she never again wanted to stand in anyone's living room but her own, selling a prospective buyer on the neighborhood and the schools. She wanted something new, something very different in her life. She had Linda, they had the house, and the future looked interesting since she, too, had spread her wings and taken a leap into the unknown.

The four of them were talking, in very early conversation, about going on vacation together. A belated, delayed double honeymoon. They'd not decided where, but were hoping to finally arrange it the following spring. As they found themselves living again, laughing, letting the immediate past move further and further away, they thought a shared vacation might be just the thing to really give them distance from it all. In the meantime, Kyle had much to do—learning to be a landlord at the building they now owned, soothing his mother's feelings over being bought out (she took the deal, knowing it was best for them all), and somehow becoming the man he had been before he ended Deidrich Keller's life. He wasn't sure that was possible, but he hoped. Death had come up to him, looked him in the eye, and walked away. It was time to live again.

AUTHOR'S NOTE

Each of the previous books has included on an "upcoming" page at the end, with sample chapters from the next adventure. In this case, I haven't yet decided what that is. The Pride Trilogy has concluded. *Death in the Headlights* (featuring Detective Linda) has come and gone. I'm not sure what's next.

It's been hinted in the epilogue that this fearless foursome go on vacation together. A holiday from hell—or to it? That's what's tickling my fancy, buzzing around in my brain. Kyle and Danny love to cruise. Linda and Kirsten have never been on one. I have a feeling they'll soon be setting sail for murder. But I can't be certain. Characters and storylines have a way of going where they want to. It's a mystery.

ABOUT THE AUTHOR

Writing is the one thing I have done consistently all my life, whether it was being expressed in short fiction, long fiction, poetry, prose, plays, or children's television scripts. It is the one thing I've always felt compelled to do. Day jobs come and go, but the keyboard is forever. One day, hopefully far in the future, they'll find me dead with my head on the space bar, having passed on to the Great Word Processor in the Sky doing what I loved to do.

Thanks to anyone and everyone who has spent some time with Kyle and the gang. I hope you'll take another ride on the mystery train, meet a new traveler or two, and keep me getting up before the sun to bring you more.

As for my personal life, I live in New York City with my husband Frank Murray and our dwindling family of cats. We have a house in the rural New Jersey countryside where we plan to move permanently someday ... maybe.

Mark McNease
www.markmcnease.com

Made in the USA
Lexington, KY
08 July 2015